LINES CROSSED

Thrilling crime fiction about a rogue detective

IAN ROBINSON

Published by The Book Folks

London, 2024

ISBN 978-1-80462-249-0

www.thebookfolks.com

LINES CROSSED is the third standalone novel in a gripping crime fiction series centring on rogue undercover cop Sam Batford. Look out for the other two, CRIMINAL JUSTICE and STATUS DRIFT.

Further details about Ian Robinson's books can be found at the back of this one.

1

Funerals. An unwanted gathering of time-pressed people full of pretensions, false charm, and platitudes. I am Detective Sergeant Sam Batford, undercover officer with the Metropolitan Police, protégé of the deceased.

Detective Superintendent Mike Hall was my boss and my partner in crime. As bosses go, he wasn't too bad. Then he bit the bullet. Literally. I was an integral part of arranging his death. Mike picked up a text message I'd arranged to be sent via an unattributable mobile phone taped to a 9mm handgun in the glove box of a car Mike was in. He got the message as he was making his bid for freedom with a criminal called Razor. Mike was shrewd. He understood that the time to do the honourable thing had come – to place the barrel of the pistol under his double-chin and pull the trigger. If he hadn't, the armed cops putting in the hard-stop of the vehicle he and Razor were in would have taken care of it for him. After all, the public frown upon criminals waving guns in front of the police.

The Met declined Mike the honour and dignity of a service burial. I stand a respectful distance away from his ex-wife, Yvonne, as well as the small police crowd. Mike's mistress has stayed clear too. A wise decision.

I found his mistress's address in his Thameside apartment when I was clearing my stuff out before the police sealed it up. I personally delivered news of his death to her, along with a verbal restraining order. Better to be safe than sorry.

I have no idea how much she knew of my business arrangements with Mike, but she assured me she'd keep her mouth shut. I know where she lives and the car she drives. Loose lips sink ships and she's keen to remain above water.

The newly appointed authorising officer for covert policing, Klara Winter, now Detective Superintendent Klara Winter of the Metropolitan Police, is the only senior officer here. My guess is she too wants to be certain that Mike's dead. I'm still in service. Same department, same role. A month ago, she ordered me to see the Met's psychologist. The psychologist knows me from previous assessments. We also have a long-standing personal agreement.

Although the session is confidential, we understand that words have consequences. If he asks how my mother is, I acknowledge she's fine, and he signs me off as fit for covert duty. In return, I leave him an ounce of cocaine at an agreed drop point. I know he's in control of his habit. He also knows a good thing when he sees it and is too shrewd to turn grass. You don't shoot your supplier when the purity of the product is quality assured by police.

Winter appealed his decision. She doesn't like me.

Not content with this, she arranged a random drugs test. I came back clean. I knew I would. I abuse the system. Nothing else. I don't blame Winter. She has a job to do. Weeding out those who shouldn't be handling large volumes of cash and drugs in the name of public protection is one of those. I'll do what it takes to protect and serve my own freedom.

The coffin has arrived. Those outside line up to follow it into the crematorium, eager to watch Mike's descent to hell. I join the paltry line, opting to sit at the back, ensuring my phones are on silent. A vicar stands up at the front and says a few words. I wasn't asked to make a speech.

The gathered mourners react in varying degrees of grief. Official words over, the curtain closes. Radiohead's *Karma Police* plays him out as he's consumed by flames. I'm numb to any emotion. As we exit, I see that the token flowers I'd arranged have been delivered. There's little sentiment in the wreath chosen from the no-thrills range of funeral foliage. The attached card contains his name only. The florist insisted something had to be written on it, if only to identify whose funeral it was for.

Winter sidles up next to me.

'How are you?'

She sounds genuine. Yes, she sent me to the mind doctor, but that was all in the name of a post-deployment review with the hope of getting rid of any bad blood. She never queried my blood returning from a statutory toxicology screening with the purity of a monk rather than the expected traces of class A drugs.

'As well as can be expected,' I reply. 'You?'

'Now that your mate, Mike, is off to pastures new, I'm ecstatic. How's your traffic attachment been?'

A snide comment in relation to my training in entry-level vehicle mechanics. All for a covert introduction into a Metropolitan Police sponsored garage on the outskirts of a North London housing estate. I had thorough training in combat vehicles in the army. I just fancied some time away from her glare. We're face to face under her umbrella as I lean towards her right ear.

'I passed with flying colours. I'm not going anywhere, and you know it, so let's get on with whatever job you want me involved in next.'

Winter smiles and in turn leans towards me. Steadying the umbrella as she does. 'As luck would have it, that's tomorrow,' she says. 'Briefing in my office, 8 a.m. Don't be late.'

She turns and steps towards Mike's widow. Fuck the wake. I have a thirst, but I refuse to share air with any of them socially. I walk back towards my car and head to my digs and an unopened bottle of Jack Daniels.

2

'Sit down, everyone.' Winter directs us to our respective seats in her new office. She's brought her throne with her from the National Crime Agency – a made-to-measure orthopaedic chair that Occupational Health approved for her. She's opted for glasses this morning. Bold frames. Next to me is DI Vince Gladwell from the Flying Squad. A career detective with the same tenacious desire for justice as Winter.

They're cut from the same cloth except Vince has a laid-back demeanour and a seventies afro to match. He's a recent transfer from the central proactive unit to the Flying Squad. We have history and he's out to make his mark, as am I.

I've been a good boy since my return from restricted duties. An internal investigation took place following the vote of no confidence given by the CPS after my last operation. An appropriate decision based on Winter's weak attempt at prosecuting me for conspiracy to murder and supplying controlled drugs.

A crime boss called Razor would have been my co-defendant had I been charged. I won't be sharing a cell with him. A case of circumstantial, but nothing substantive, as far as my evidence went. So, here we are – one happy family sat around a meeting table in a clinical-looking office in New Scotland Yard, ready to tackle another criminal network.

I feel a state of unease at the regime change. On previous occasions, Mike would have held this meeting in the small side room off the main UCO office. Now it feels like a summons to the headmistress.

Winter clears her throat. 'I'll dispense with introductions as DI Gladwell informs me you know each other. DI Gladwell, you may state what you require from my department in terms of resources. As I explained on the phone, they are small to non-existent. I cannot commit to a long-term deployment of any kind. I hope you understand. Times have changed. Covert policing is under review within the service. As of now, I have DS Batford and one other UC currently deployed on your operation, courtesy of an outside force. They are running late because of operational commitments, but will be here shortly.'

It's good to be back on the front line where I belong. I've been in the role of office manager long enough to consider resigning.

Vince leans down and takes out three identical orange dockets from a briefcase on the floor. He hands them out. Each one is marked "Secret".

'These dockets provide a detailed briefing of our targets and what we've ascertained from lifestyle surveillance,' he says. 'They commit traditional armed robberies. No frills. Get in, get the job done, and get out. They choose their targets well and take no prisoners.'

He pauses, checks we're all attentive, then continues.

'The last three robberies have been on security vans carrying cash. They're strapping machine pistols and handguns for good measure. They're surveillance-aware and a bitch to keep up with. They regularly switch vehicles. We're struggling to know what transport they're using or where they're laid up. Our plan is to put DS Batford in a flat on the estate where they live. We've already set up a garage nearby that's being operated from by another UC. DS Batford will work with the UC from there. We're hoping DS Batford can get the targets' attention, enough to trust him to work their cars and store them at the garage. It's the only option we have. The flat's good to go. DS Batford just needs to move in.'

My gut constricts at the sound of sharing the streets with another UC. I don't like it. Never have. I have other "work" to do. Work that isn't compatible with legal detective duties.

Winter's desk phone rings. She answers it. 'Yes … Yes, come in.' She puts it down and all eyes turn to the door.

Mine widen at the person standing in the doorway. It cannot be. I get up and look at Winter then back at Kat Mills who walks into the room. It's as if everyone's in on the joke apart from me. My mind's spinning. My heart thumps against my chest. She's in my world again and with the requisite access card and vetting. I waste no time in letting them know my feelings on the subject. The last time I saw her, she was seconded to the Met from another undercover unit to act as an enforcer for Razor. It was by chance that I discovered this.

'What in the love of fuck is she doing here?' I bellow as she enters the office. I put out a hand to block her path. She's having none of it.

'Put your hand down. I've no wish to dance, so can we sit? My journey was terrible and I'm dying for a coffee.' She eases past me and sits in a spare chair.

Vince is staring in confusion and Winter has a wry smile that I just wish would fade the fuck away.

'I need to take a piss.' I step through the office door into the corridor and crash through the door opposite and into the gents. I'm the only customer. Winter is clever, using an outside force to supply the UC. This UC knows how I work. I'm a marked man in Winter's eyes. I turn to the sink and run the cold tap. I cup my hands, fill them with water, and douse my face.

The main door opens and Vince steps in. He stands at the urinal and sniffs. 'You know Holly then?' He's looking up at the walls as his piss splashes the porcelain.

'How long has she been on this job?' I ask.

Vince zips up and strolls over to the sink, checking his appearance in the mirror. 'A few months. She's been working the garage, but none of the vermin are interested in the cheese. We need new bait and that's you.'

He looks at me in the mirror. 'You need to get your shit together. I've got a dedicated squad of seasoned detectives looking to take this lot down. Dry your hands and let's wrap this meeting up and get to work. You never kept in touch since I left the covert world, which was disappointing. Now we've got a chance to mix things up again. Let's get on board and enjoy the good old days, eh?'

Vince dries his hands, pulls down the linen towel to a clean section, and leaves. His brown, leather, three-quarter length coat slaps the door as he exits.

I check myself in the mirror. I need a shave.

Winter has played her ace card at the wrong time in a game that she should have folded on long ago; in fact, she shouldn't have even approached the table. Holly was on my last job. I believe she was put there by Winter to target me and Mike. Winter may think she's had the last laugh, but this game will only have one winner. Me.

I exit the toilet and go straight into Winter's office. I can sense Holly and Vince watching me as I walk to the window that overlooks Victoria Embankment. 'It was a shock seeing her again. Let's carry on.' I sit back in my chair, eyes on Winter.

'"Her" is DC Holly Burns, a UC from Manchester. Ignorance like that won't be tolerated by me, DS Batford. Take the docket and liaise with DI Gladwell. I'm overseeing the entire covert operation. I'll let the commander know the paperwork is in place and ready to sign off.' Winter looks over her glasses and we all take the hint to leave.

It's strange seeing Winter in New Scotland Yard – a place I considered my impenetrable domain.

I've underestimated her detective abilities. I'd heard of the other candidates for her job here and they all had impressive careers. She's more self-assured now. I get the sense she would enjoy seeing my head revolving on a post outside Scotland Yard.

I block the image and focus on Vince, who is in the corridor speaking to Holly.

Vince breaks his conversation and turns to me. 'Head to Victoria. I know a place we can talk,' he says.

'Why now? What's the panic?' I say.

He gives me a stare I remember from our undercover days. He's a solid guy and at six foot four, quite imposing. He never suffered fools and always carried off whatever role he performed to great effect. For the first time since my arrest, I feel nervous.

'I've got a team hungry for results. Save the attitude for the villains,' he says. I smile and he reciprocates with a display of teeth that look like they've had work. He slaps me on the back.

The force is significant. Message delivered.

Holly grabs her bag from the floor and makes no comment. Her focus is on her phone. My focus is on survival.

Sensitive log entry 1

Sensitive decision log for Detective Superintendent Klara Winter – Operation Envy.

10th September, 0800 hours

I have accepted a request for covert resources from DI Vince Gladwell of the Flying Squad. He has intelligence concerning several subjects with access to firearms committing cash-in-transit robberies within the jurisdiction of the Metropolitan Police.

DI Gladwell has requested the use of a male undercover officer to assist in the gathering of evidence concerning serious organised crime. A female undercover officer from an outside force is currently deployed on the operation.

I'm a month into my new role as authorising officer for covert policing after transferring from the National Crime Agency. It's evident that the current covert resources in the Metropolitan Police are incredibly thin. A glut of resignations from undercover officers has left a serious shortage of trained and suitable staff. DS Batford fits the profile sought by DI Gladwell. DS Batford is currently performing the role of office manager. I placed him in this position as I have had reservations about his suitability to perform effectively as an undercover officer since his last deployment – a deployment my NCA team were engaged in. However, the Met's psychologist deems him fit for covert duty.

Mindful of the current staff shortages, I also assigned him to a basic vehicle mechanics and familiarisation course, which he has completed. The training was commensurate with his role, and as luck would have it, will be helpful on this operation. I thought it only covered basic mechanics, however DS Batford informed me he was also assessed as competent in the fitting, maintenance, and retrieval of covert trackers and listening devices within vehicles. This wasn't an aspect of the training I was aware of. The command has a team for this purpose – a team I will continue to use.

I still have concerns about DS Batford's honesty and integrity. However, despite intensive investigation, there is nothing to corroborate any suspicion of corruption. I'm noting this should any evidence of corruption surface during this investigation. Ideally, I'd seek another officer from an outside force, but can't justify this due to budget constraints; especially as DS Batford was cleared as fit for duty by the psychologist.

I've briefed DI Gladwell as to my concerns. He has previous working knowledge of DS Batford in a covert capacity. He assures me DS Batford will be managed.

I admire his optimism. Commander Helen Barnes authorises DS Batford's use as a covert human intelligence source for this operation. I'll be overseeing covert resources, and DI Gladwell and his team will be overseen by his command.

A briefing will take place tomorrow where DS Batford will be handed over to DI Gladwell for the purposes of this operation. I'm satisfied with the work of the current UC. They will support each other while deployed.

Entry complete.

Klara Winter – Detective Superintendent
Covert Policing
Authorising Officer
Op Envy

3

I remember this café. It was one of Mike's haunts when he wanted time out of the office. The coffee house is small with minimal seating and has a basement that can be used as a meeting room. I'm sitting with Holly and Vince around a small table in a comfy chair, sipping a latte. How times have changed from roadside vans and instant coffee. Vince puts his tall glass of one shot with extra foam down on the table. He's ready to start our briefing.

'I need you both on the same page for this work. I don't give a shit what happened on the last job. You're on mine now, and that's what counts,' he says. 'This crew is street-educated. They evolved from a gang lifestyle. When it comes to violence, they're mindless. The last driver who stood up to them got a face full of acid. Bottom line is, we can't stay ahead of the game with them. Holly's been fronting the garage, but they haven't taken the option of coming in. It was a long shot. I thought they may see it as an opportunity to have their cars stored or work done on them. They prefer to use nicked ones and dump them after. I need to convince them to hang on to one. That way we can get technical on the cars, making tracking them easier when they're out.' He takes a drink.

Winter has played a strong game. Holly nearly had me fooled until our last outing. Sadly, her tradecraft let her down. The outline of a warrant card, where it had been carried in her jeans pocket, revealed all I needed to know to confirm she was like me. She can handle herself though, which could be an advantage. She's strong on gathering evidence, and that's where I'm nervous. She played Razor like a well-tuned fiddle.

In the end, we were all dancing to her jig. Now we are sitting together as operatives on the same job. This job is different from our last venture. I have a flat to crash in, on an estate where the crew live and the parties last twenty-four hours. Some undercover officers like to drop by covert premises for appearance's sake. Not me. I enjoy being among the enemy.

Holly looks across at Vince. 'I've done my best in that shithole,' she says. 'If they're not interested, they're not interested. I've been up to my eyes in oil and grease. I've been on the estate, showing my face, when the targets are on the block. It's not been the easiest of gigs.'

Vince leans in, palms out in front. 'There's no criticism from me. It's been a tough ask. This lot aren't stupid. If they were, they'd be banged up. We've lost community support. This lot control the estate. The amount of people willing to talk has dropped. Talking to police isn't worth the risk to them. It's back to basics.'

Good old-fashioned policing. Oh, how I've missed thee. I'm looking forward to kicking back with Vince. His squad consists of the best of the best – any dead wood cleaned out. He cherry-picks his people well.

Winter's threat of a return to uniform policing was weak management. She underestimates the good that's done at grassroots level. How boots on the ground breed intelligence. Intelligence that's lacking on this operation. Would I go back to pounding the beat? No fucking way.

Vince's unity speech has come to an end. He's moved on to the job.

'Each docket contains a profile of the main targets. Winter refers to them as "subjects". I'm not Winter. There's three targets. They're as tight as a noose and shifty as hell. Warrants have been executed on their homes in the last five months. Each address was clean. I need you to get their attention. I know you can do it. All the details are in those orange dockets. Holly, you're taking on Sam as an extra pair of hands. I've arranged for some seizures from Traffic to be brought to the garage to make it look busy. I'm not trying to interfere with your approach. I need the main players on board with the cars. Sam, Winter will be paying all your expenses, I've no control over it. Same for you, Holly. Don't take the piss.'

Vince sits back, chuckling. He knows it will hurt me going to Winter for cash. He hands me a set of keys and an address to a flat on the estate. He reaches into his coat and produces a plain white envelope with my name on it.

'Winter told me to give you this.' He places it on the table. I don't recognise the handwriting on the front.

'Get to grips with the target profiles in the docket,' Vince continues, 'then we'll get started. Any updates through me. I'll talk with Winter. My DS will be busy with the outside team so contact me with any issues and updates. You know the score, people. You've got ten minutes with those files. I need to be elsewhere.'

'Have you not got another DS on the team who can cover?' Holly says, perplexed.

'Welcome to the Met, Holly. Understaffed, under budget, and underpaid,' says Vince.

I open the docket. Toots, Sugar, and Nines are the main targets. All in their early twenties with previous convictions for robbery. They were on the same prison block in Feltham Young Offenders, but for different crimes. Seems they got on so well they wanted to stay in touch once they were released. A bromance like no other. I memorise the recent surveillance pictures.

Toots and Nines are black guys, Toots being the stockier and taller of the two. Sugar is a white fella, average height, with a shaved head and a scar on his left cheek. Toots and Nines are the main men while Sugar handles the wheels.

Drugs are mentioned too, but not in the volumes I'm used to taking out.

It will be difficult getting to know these boys enough to be involved in anything beyond working their cars. I'm the wrong age for socialising with them. I'll have to provide something they can't access, if I'm to be of use.

I'm acutely aware that Vince knows undercover tactics. He wants this team banged up with no headaches when it comes to evidence. Winter will want the same. What do I want out of it? A clean sheet – not from crime, from Winter. Winter has an issue; that issue is me. She'll stop at nothing until she sees her theory that I'm corrupt proved correct.

This outing is making me nervous for other reasons too. Three to be exact: Holly, Vince, and Winter. The bad guys I don't have a problem with. No matter how much the police big them up, they will fall. It's part of my work satisfaction guarantee.

The cops I'm working with are a different matter. Winter has recruited a solid team. Any one of them would stamp out a corrupt cop faster than they could cuff him.

The only bracelet I willingly wear is a string one given to me by a monk in Bali. I don't think he blessed it enough. If he knew the bad karma I'm reaping, he'd be on the next plane to retrieve it.

I put down the docket and open the sealed white envelope. It's from Yvonne, Mike's widow. She must have given it to Winter at the funeral. Why she didn't hand it to me, I don't know. Vince and Holly are in conversation and leaving me to it. I take out the letter. All it contains is an address and time: 1800 hours today. I place it in my jacket pocket. I have time before I need to be there.

'You had long enough?' Vince says, with a tone of voice that implies I have.

I push the file back to him. 'Plenty. When do I start?'

'You start as of now. I've given you the keys to the flat you've been allocated on the estate. Come up with your own cover story as to why you're there. Holly is using the previous pseudonym of Kat for this job, and you'll use Sky. You'll be each other's cover officer for this one. Good luck, stay in touch, and don't do anything I wouldn't do.'

With that, Vince leaves.

The atmosphere is menacing. Neither of us knows where we truly stand with each other. I don't trust Holly, and I sense she doesn't trust me.

I break the silence.

'What car have you got?' I ask.

She looks back in my direction. 'I don't have one. I've used public transport to the garage.'

'Finish your drink and let's get our transport sorted.'

I get up. Kat does too, leaving what remains of her coffee.

* * *

'Do you ever come out from under a motor, or have you developed an oil-sniffing habit?' I say into the void of the inspection pit under the car.

Little Chris, who controls the covert fleet at our Lambeth garages, crawls out of the pit and unfurls his lanky, six-foot-seven frame to stand up. I shake his hand and introduce Holly.

'We need two motors. Nothing too flash but fitting for a garage owner and their mechanic. The garage is on the edge of a North London housing estate.'

Little Chris scratches his oil-grimed temple as his eyes scan the basement area. 'You've caught me at a bad time for vehicles, Sam. We've lost a few, thanks to you.'

He makes a fair point.

'No time is a good time for the covert fleet manager when it comes to loaning out cars. You must have something,' I say.

His eyes widen as he wags his index finger inches from his face.

'Thinking about it,' he says, 'I do have a couple of cars that would fit. Not what you usually like, but it's the best at short notice. A Mini Cooper S and John Cooper Works, both six years old. Flash, but not too flash.'

'I'll take the Works. Holly, you've got the S,' I say.

Holly raises her eyebrows and crosses her arms. 'Not so fast, sunshine. I'm the owner of the garage and you're my gofer. You get the S. I get the Works.'

I don't care either way. Let her have this win. I have every intention of blagging my own transport away from the police fleet.

'Suit yourself,' I say.

She smiles and walks over to the Works car. It's British racing green, unlike the Cooper S, which is black with a chequered roof. Little Chris leaves to get the paperwork.

'I have a meeting to attend,' I say, 'so I'll be off. I'll get settled into the flat tonight. What time are you opening the garage tomorrow?'

'Eight. Bring used overalls, and I like my coffee milky with one sugar.'

Little Chris returns with the papers and I sign off on the Cooper S, taking the keys.

'Hey, Chris, you got any spare overalls?'

He points to his office. 'In there. Various sizes for the other mechanics. Find one that fits, and I'll replace it.'

I leave to find a set that's suitably covered in oil and grime. If I'm to be her gofer I'll have to look like I've done some work and I need Holly to think I'm being compliant.

By the time I return from a clothing hunt, Holly is signed off too. I sling the overalls in the back of my car. We both start up our engines and head through the winding ramps up to the surface and away to our respective areas of work. I'm looking forward to a fresh start, away from the confines of the office.

4

I've stayed in some dives before, but this flat surpasses them all. The soles of my boots stick to the drab linoleum floor of the hall that appears to continue throughout the flat. I take solace in knowing my stay isn't permanent, unlike the other poor sods who live on the estate. The estate is on the Holloway and Hornsey border. A clash of the classes if ever there was one. A seven-storey, 1970s eyesore. My journey from lift to door was closely observed from various points on the long balconies, runways facilitating access to the flats. At ground level, in an effort to offset any sense of imprisonment, the planners added a token green space.

A set of swings drifts back and forth in the breeze. They are the only intact parts of the play area. The rest looks as though it's been caught in the aftermath of an explosion. Graffiti provides the only splashes of colour in an open concrete casket.

I bolt the flat's door from the inside and draw the remnants of a net curtain that barely covers a small, mottled-glass pane set in the door. Off the hall to the left is a compact kitchenette. Straight ahead is a lounge, bathroom, and one bedroom.

I dump my bag of meagre belongings and wonder if I can find enough paint to cover the purple living room walls. There was a time when I'd arrive at my flop address and Mike would have left a bottle of Scotch and a local takeout menu. He wasn't all bad.

The sound of a heavy bass makes the living room window vibrate. Welcome to the hood. I check my watch. I have two hours until my meeting with Yvonne. I grab my jacket, phones, and leave.

* * *

I check the address in the envelope. I'm at the right one. The words "The Salon" wink at me in red neon from above the doorway. I wait on the opposite side of the road and observe. The place is busy.

A young lad sweeps the floor while a trio of staff pamper their patrons. I don't recognise any of them.

The clientele appear relaxed. There is no one I would consider hostile or a risk to me. My hair has grown out since it was last shaved off. I'm in two minds whether to let it continue or go with a number one all over. Although this is a private matter, I'm aware that I could be watched. I'm mindful of my tradecraft. It would cost lives if I wasn't.

I'm intrigued to go ahead with the meet. Everyone I've targeted, bar one, is in prison or dead. A chair looks like it will become free when the stylist holds a mirror up behind the client's head and moves it around for a last check. I cross over and enter.

A bell announces my arrival. The stylist, now at the till, takes the payment and, as her client leaves, she smiles in my direction.

'Have you booked?' she asks, maintaining the smile with obvious practice.

'I have an appointment at six with Yvonne.'

She scans down the page and picks up a phone on the desk. 'Your six is here. Where do you want him?' She listens, then puts the phone down. 'Through here.'

She leads and I follow her to a door at the back.

It's a standard internal door that can't be locked. She knocks and a female voice tells her to come in.

She pushes the door and invites me to go ahead, which I do.

'Do you want a drink? I can offer tea or coffee – nothing stronger,' the stylist says.

'Whatever's good,' I say.

She leaves.

Yvonne's shoulder-length brown hair is tied up in a bun, the subtle tone of which mirrors her bottle-tanned skin.

'Take a seat, Sam. I won't bite,' she says.

I perch on the edge of a single leather tub chair, and she occupies a matching seat. The door opens. The girl who showed me in brings in a pot of tea and a cafetière, then leaves.

Yvonne pours me a coffee. 'I'll be mum. You never were any good at social etiquette, bless you.'

She looks tired. It's no wonder, having to live with Mike. And I use "live with" loosely. He used every excuse in the book to be at work.

'So, how have you been?' I say, tentatively.

'Top of the world, love. Mike's death couldn't have come at a better time. I'm not stupid, Sam. I know he had a bit on the side. At least she had the common sense to stay away from the funeral.' She sits back and sips her drink.

I say nothing and mirror her drinking. I'm here for one thing: to know why she left the note with Winter. She must have read my mind.

'Sorry for the cryptic message, but it was the only way of getting hold of you. You don't keep a number long and the last one I could find was dead. I didn't know if I'd see much of you, so I thought it was easier to leave the envelope with your boss. I hope it didn't cause you any problems.'

She gets up and goes to her desk where she opens a drawer and brings out a wooden box and a large brown envelope. 'These are for you, from Mike. He'd made a will, and you were in it. I made him do it once he started investing the money. We're taken care of. I made sure of that. Our solicitor knows the score too, so you don't have to see her either.'

She slides the box over with the envelope on top. I don't touch them.

'You can open them. I know what's in them.' She takes out a cigarette and offers me one.

I decline.

'Save me the effort, Yvonne, and tell me what's in them. You've gone through a lot of theatre for a couple of items you could have told me about at the funeral or given me there.'

She smiles and accepts my offer to light her cigarette. Her hands shake slightly. She takes a drag and blows out the smoke.

'The box contains his ashes. He didn't leave instructions for where he wanted scattering, so I'll leave that up to you. I'm sure you had a favourite haunt you both enjoyed. You can dump him there as far as I'm concerned.'

Charming. After all we'd been through, he leaves me his dust.

'And the envelope?' I say.

The cigarette quivers between her index and middle finger.

'He was a bastard, Sam, but he did have a heart even if he had a strange way of showing it. I know all about the central London pad he had and how he got it. We had no secrets, Sam. Despite our estranged appearance, he trusted me – he loved me. My lips are sealed. It wouldn't do me any good to talk to your lot and I've no intention of doing that.'

I keep my breathing steady while I assess her body language. On the surface, she would appear to be telling the truth. I surmise she's done well out of our criminal activities. She has a lifestyle she'll want to maintain. The salon is all a front. A legitimate business with average takings for the area. Mike will have made sure the main money was protected for them both. It would make sense for him to keep her onside. Yvonne isn't stupid, and Mike knew it.

'The Thameside flat wasn't the only property he had,' she continues. 'He only revealed what he could lose. The London pad was one of the things he was prepared to let the police seize. That's why he invited you there. He had property abroad. Property he was hoping to capitalise on with Razor. That's gone. I have a country house he left me. Nothing fancy, more of a cottage in Kent, but it's what I wanted. There was one other property though, and now it belongs to you. The deeds and keys are all in that envelope. The lifestyle caught up with him in the end. He'd been on the take for years, well before meeting you. He was preparing to leave us all, Sam. That's why I made him do the will. If he hadn't, then it would have all been lost.'

She carries on smoking and scratches her newly manicured thumbnail with her index finger. 'He didn't tell you everything, Sam. Let's just leave it at that,' she says. Now she's about to cry.

I get up and take Mike and the envelope.

'He's still heavy even in this state,' I say.

She stifles a laugh, but the tears flow.

Time to leave.

'I'll see myself out. I hope the rest of your life treats you better than he did.' There's nothing more to say.

'Aren't you forgetting something?' she says, waving a set of clippers. 'You never know who's watching.'

Even she was drilled in the craft. What a miserable life she must lead.

I sit down, and she runs the blades over my head. Once she's finished, I exit the salon and return to my car. London's skyline has gone dark and so must I.

I place Mike in the footwell of the Mini and wedge my jacket against the box to stop it moving. I check my surroundings in the mirrors. The streets have not changed since I parked up. None of the cars that were here when I arrived have moved. Foot traffic is light. I put on the radio and Interpol's song, *Surveillance*, comes on to fill the void.

I make a conscious decision not to look in the envelope or go to my newly inherited, money-laundered abode. Mike managed to find a bent solicitor to keep it all clean. That's one thing to be thankful to him for.

The traffic on the Holloway Road is crawling.

My attention is drawn to a cash-in-transit van parked outside Sainsbury's.

There's the roar of an engine. Pedestrians start darting for cover as a red VW Golf GTI shifts from the line in front of me and brakes hard. The front passenger door flings open, and a masked occupant leaps out.

A guard steps out of Sainsbury's, box in hand, and the masked robber smashes the butt of a gun into his back. The guard doubles over, desperately clinging to the cash box. Both rear doors to the Golf open and two more robbers alight, carrying Czech-made Škorpion automatic weapons. People scatter. Drivers bail out of their cars and run away from the Golf. I remain where I am, casually observing the drama.

The guard gives up the box when the barrel of a gun is pointed at his helmet. A robber throws the box into the back of the Golf.

The cash-in-transit driver sits still, hands over his head, avoiding eye contact. Idiots on the footway have phones out pointing in the direction of the robbery, but the gang doesn't care – their faces are covered by Anonymous masks.

A loud explosion causes alarms in shops to start ringing and pedestrians to duck for cover. I'd not been paying attention to the back of the van, which is now rocking under the force of the blast, its rear doors blown open.

As the smoke clears, a robber alights through the gloom carrying two more boxes and throws those into the Golf. The robbers get back in the car and they're away, across the pavement and onto a clearer section of road.

The wail of sirens pierces the air. A minute later, the uniform response is at the scene. All that's left for them is the injured guard sat on the kerb, helmet off, head hung low. The van smoulders as a fire engine pulls up and several firefighters begin tackling the driver's door. The driver, unable to exit due to the internal security system, will probably be terrified.

I look at the wooden box in the footwell of the Mini. 'Fuck me Mike, it's all kicked off out here.'

I don't wait around. As far as I'm concerned, I saw nothing. The execution of the robbery was impressive. They had clearly observed the van's route and timed the job well. I'm surmising they were aware that it'd picked up cash at earlier stops. They'd let the van run to gain more from the job.

It's a high-risk gamble with CCTV and increased armed police patrols. There used to be plain-clothes police who shadowed the vans as a crime-prevention exercise. No longer so. Cuts have consequences. I have no idea of the robbers' ethnicity, age, or sex. I only have the colour and registration number of the car, which will either have been stolen or is running with false plates. I log that in my mind.

5

I head towards Highgate Hill, passing the Whittington Hospital. I'm on the bridge over the Archway Road. There's a girl sat on the edge of the wall on the other side of a safety barrier.

I stop the car and get out. The road over the bridge is narrow, but people can move round me or wait.

No one's interested.

I've been in this dark place. It's not a time for an unwelcome do-gooder shouting "Don't do it."

She sits on the wall, hands behind her.

I get out, leaving the car door open so as not to shock her if she hears it shut. I make as quiet an approach as I can. The engines of passing traffic drown my footfalls. I intend to get close enough, so she'll know I'm there, but not close enough to startle her.

I lean against the bars of the barrier. I'm far enough away not to spook her. The amber glow of an overhead street lamp illuminates us. The safety barrier is at least eight feet tall and is needed because so many jump from here; it is locally known as "Suicide Bridge". I don't know how she's managed to breach it, but she has. The vertical bars that separate us make me feel like an unwanted visitor at a zoo.

On noticing me, she freezes. Her feet dangle over the edge of the wall.

'Don't come anywhere near me, do you hear? I'll jump if you do, so back off,' she says, vehement in her tone.

I respect her request and remain where I am. Cars using the bridge are slowing now. Headlights clash with dots of light from phone cameras. In minutes, her final moment of desperation will be preserved on a stranger's phone — recorded with the single purpose of harvesting likes and shares via social media. It's a sick world.

'I can't come closer, the bars are stopping me,' I say.

She swings her legs. Her untied shoe drops, and she watches it fall. It bounces off the roof of a lorry before ending up under the wheels of one behind it.

'Oh well, I won't be needing shoes where I'm going.'

She turns her head towards me. She looks no older than seventeen. Lank, dark brown hair sticks against her forehead. She is wearing what was once a white denim jacket, now stained with dirt. Mascara lines her pale cheeks in tear-streaked strokes. She removes her jacket and drops it over the edge.

Car horns resound from the road below. A male voice shouts, 'Do it, you crazy bitch, and save us all some money!'

I look over the edge of the bridge at the male who shouted, sat with a pint outside a pub. White guy, early fifties, England football top, and jeans. He's never seen the inside of a gym. The light from the pub captures him in his one-man play. My attention is drawn back to the girl as she edges closer to the end of the wall. The road below, one push away.

'Where are you from?' I say, as a way of distracting her.

She's not impressed with my efforts at negotiation. Buying drugs and guns is one thing. Talking a person out of suicide is another. One I'm confident with, but in this situation I haven't a clue.

'Why do you want to know? Are you another one who thinks I'm draining your country of precious funds? I was forced here. Promised a new life. A secure future. Instead, I ended up getting pimped to men like you to have fun with and tossed away when I served no other purpose.' Tears fill her eyes. She's shivering.

She looks back and forth between the road below and me. As she turns away, I inch closer.

'I didn't mean it like that. Where do you sleep? I might be able to help.' It's a weak attempt at reconciliation.

I'm distracted by the sounds of feet behind me. It's a uniform officer walking towards where I'm stood. Another is unfurling police crime-scene tape across the road. More cops are arriving below. There are no sirens announcing their arrival, just the pulsing blue strobes of the roof lights.

As I turn back from the officer, the girl lifts her head. She gently pushes her hair back from her forehead. The last time I saw that look in someone's eyes was in the army barracks right before they blew their brains out.

'Thanks for stopping,' she says to me in a quiet voice. 'It's the first time I've felt seen.'

Before I can reach out, she's gone. My world slows. There's a heavy crunch of glass followed by the sound of expelled, forced air. People are screaming. There's an almighty noise of falling masonry. I instinctively duck. The uniform officer does the same. She grabs her hat and inches towards me in a crouch.

'Are you okay?' she says.

Her hand is on my shoulder, and I start to stand up. Looking over the bridge, the full horror of the scene comes into view. The girl's torso is embedded in the window of a lorry. Her legs droop at strange angles over the front of the lorry's cab. Her jeans are soaked in blood. Her right, shoeless, foot is motionless.

The lorry driver must have lost control as she hit the windscreen and landed in his lap. I assume he applied the brakes hard, and this was the sound of expelled air I heard. Not being able to see, he went straight through the front of the pub. The frontage is totalled.

The pithy excuse of manhood that was sitting outside shouting abuse has joined his foe in death – his head crushed under the nearside wheel of the lorry. In the distance are more blue lights. Too many, too late, to stop the traffic below the bridge and prevent her death. I'm jolted back from the macabre scene by a calm female voice.

'Don't look anymore,' the officer says, 'you'll never forget it. I'll need to take a statement while I'm here. Nothing to fear, just procedure. I don't think you'll be required at the coroner's court. I witnessed her jump. I just want to know about any conversation beforehand, her state of mind, that kind of thing. Did you know her?'

'No. The conversation was one-sided, despite me trying to engage her. I won't be helpful.'

She taps out my bland statement on her iPad. Conscious of the crowd that's gathered, I don't tell her I'm police. I give her a card with my true ID and a PO box number. The estate where I'll be staying is nearby. Anyone could be listening. I electronically sign the statement and she lets me go. All very clinical. A life reduced to a case number.

6

As I enter the estate, watchers gather on the various landings. I sense their gaze following me through the block's doors and picking me up again as I exit the lift and walk along the landing towards my flat.

A pale-faced youth takes a drag on a cigarette and shifts his attention to me. He moves away from the edge of the landing wall and blocks my path. I'm hoping the password to continue is a simple "Hello." He looks me up and down as I get closer.

'Where do you think you're going?' he says.

'Home. You?'

'I haven't seen you before.'

He makes the mistake of maintaining my gaze. I'm like a dog in that respect: never stare at me. You can't predict how I'll behave under threat.

'I live in the flat you're standing in front of,' I tell him. 'Do you have a welcome basket of home-baked goods?'

He moves in closer.

I have my keys in my hand with the Yale protruding through my index and middle fingers in a loose grip. He's unaware of this as he's still in a staring contest. I'm done with his floor show.

'Look,' I say, 'you have two options: move aside so I can get in or take a dive off the landing. Either way, I'm going inside.'

His eyes shift towards the edge of the balcony. He can tell I'm serious. A good sign. A neighbour exits her flat pushing a buggy with an unstrapped toddler inside. My door blocker walks away, making the sign of a pistol as he leaves.

I've arrived. Home sweet home. Rumours will travel about a stranger moving in. That suits me. I need my presence felt. I bolt the door to the flat and flop down on a torn, two-seat sofa. A low bass thumps a muffled beat from next door. A couple starts rowing from the upstairs flat. The water-stained ceiling shudders as tempered feet test the plaster. The erratic rhythm is broken by the sound of skin on skin and the wail of a female in distress. A door slams. The party's over.

I can hear a woman crying over the sound of the music. At least I know she's conscious and breathing. The assailant must have been the one to leave. I pick my bag from the floor, open it, and lay out an assortment of phones and SIM cards. I get them ready to roll. I fold a bundle of notes – four twenties held together by one twenty-pound note folded over them – the way of the drugs trade.

My work phone rings. It's Holly.

'You good?' she says.

'If by good you mean caught between a rave and a domestic, then I'm the best I've ever been.'

'That bad, eh?'

'What's up?'

'Charming. Can't I call to make sure a colleague's okay on his first evening in new digs?' she says.

'Sorry. Mike wasn't one for concern. I'll be at the garage by eight.'

'Sure. I'm looking forward to you making me tea and bringing me spanners,' Holly says, laughing.

Laughter. An unusual sound in my world. It makes me uneasy. I'm aware she's trying to be amenable.

With Mike gone, I feel alone. I must survive on my wits and guile or end up in prison.

'Look, I appreciate the call. I'll see you tomorrow and we'll go from there,' I say.

She grunts and hangs up.

* * *

I'm glad to get away from my estate. I didn't sleep well. The earlier screams of pain from the neighbours were replaced with cries of joy as they reconciled.

I arrive at the garage. The front grill to the unit opens and I drive my Mini onto a ramp. I pop the bonnet for effect and go to a small kitchen area. As I wait for the kettle to boil, I swap my clean T-shirt for a dirtier one, and grab the overalls I'm to wear. I'm startled by a cough. It's Holly in the doorway. She looks away as I pull the top half of the overalls over my torso.

She'll have clocked the marks and scars on my back despite my best efforts to disguise them with a large tattoo depicting Jos A. Smith's *The Priest of Dark Flight*.

She's dressed in overalls, ready for work.

'Didn't mean to startle you. I didn't know you'd be getting undressed.' She pours boiling water into the cups I'd prepared.

'No worries,' I say. I point to a fire-exit door. Outside, we won't be recorded by the garage's covert system. She carries the mugs, and we leave. A mound of old tyres acts as a rest area. I take a seat and turn to Holly.

'So, what's the average day like?'

'For the most part, answering the phone. Otherwise it's pretty quiet,' she says, tilting her chin towards the sun.

'I had a run-in with an estate regular. Didn't come to anything, but he made it known, by a gun gesture, he'll be back,' I say.

'I don't want a war here.' She raises her glasses, as if her eyes would tell me more than her mouth just has.

'I've no intention of starting any war. I'm updating my cover officer with information on an adverse encounter.'

'Look, I'm sorry. It's just that I've had one bum job after another since the one we were on. I need this one to get started. I struggle with Winter and Vince thinking I'm incapable of attracting the attention we need.' She turns towards the sun. Glasses back over her eyes.

'It has nothing to do with your abilities as a UC. It's the tactics that aren't working. I attract attention. It's part of my personality. How I do that is open to debate. It's all about control with Winter. If she can feel the choke chain tighten, she's happy.'

'You give her credit for nothing, do you?' Holly says.

'I give her credit for getting where she has in the job,' I say.

'Bollocks do you. Women work twice as hard to get the recognition we deserve. Now make me another cuppa. Milk, two sugars.' Holly gives me a clipped smile, passing me her empty mug.

7

The throaty sound of a car's engine breaks my concentration. I look up from under the Mini's bonnet as a dark-blue BMW reverses towards the open garage doors. It's been an uneventful day and we're ready to down tools.

The vehicle stops, and the engine remains running. The rear doors open. The male I'd confronted outside my flat steps out. Another gets out the nearside. A wheel brace I'd placed under the bonnet of the Mini is within my reach as they approach.

Holly comes over.

'Can I help you?' she says, wiping her hands on a rag.

'It's him I want to see,' the landing goon says.

His minder hangs back.

This is going to end well. The type of clientele we want to attract have arrived.

'What do you want?' I say.

'I'm here to give you the message you chose to ignore last night.' He is at the nearside of the Mini. The reflection in the two-way mirror which forms a window to our makeshift office, tells me he's carrying a blade in his back pocket. I'm conscious that everything in here is being covertly recorded.

'We're about to close, so be quick,' I say.

Laughing, he turns to his shadow. 'I told you he was deaf.' His attention is back on me now. 'Thing is, you made threats I wasn't happy with. You were lucky that girl and her kid came out or I'd have done you,' he says.

I lean in and whisper, 'Look, it's only my second day. I need this job. Can we take this elsewhere?'

He's having none of it. 'You were seen talking to the filth last night on Suicide Bridge. That ain't cool.' This revelation comes as a welcome surprise. It demonstrates how strong the control of the estate is and how they protect it from people they don't know. People like me.

'That? I had no choice. I'd just seen a girl jump to her death. What your grass didn't tell you is that the name and address I gave the officer was bullshit.'

He's not buying it. 'You spoke to the copper and that ain't cool,' he says. 'We owned that bitch who went over the edge. My people are nervous that the cops will be sniffing all over our manor. That's on you. You owe us.'

He's serious. I'm sensing he also has a solution to how I can pay my debt.

'Wrong place, wrong time, for me,' I say. 'I don't owe anyone anything. You've heard my side.'

Holly remains a passive observer, but I know she'll be making her own assessment.

'If you know what's good for you, you'll shut the fuck up,' he says. 'If you carry on like you are, you're a dead man.'

Holly steps in. 'Look, I don't know what he's done, but I don't want any trouble. Why don't you let us look at your BMW? It sounds like the exhaust has a hole in it. We'll do the repair for nothing. What happens outside of here, with him, I don't care about.'

'We'll be back,' he says. They stroll back to the car.

I make an obvious play at taking a better look in the driver's mirror. I see who's in the hot seat. The scar down his right cheek is a dead giveaway. It's Sugar.

They get in and the BMW leaves.

'Did you see the driver?' Holly says, ruffling her cropped hair.

'It was Sugar. I'm certain of it. Hopefully, the camera picked him up. I'll ask Vince to get the footage checked. See if anything's useful,' I say.

Holly nods. 'So, what was all that about? Who was this girl you were with?' There's a stentorian tone to her voice.

'She was on Archway Bridge. I was on my way to the flat. It was obvious she was looking to jump, so I tried to talk her out of it. She ended up through the windscreen of a lorry. Uniform turned up. I told them what I saw and gave them my correct details. That's the sum of it,' I say, hoping the garage recording will note I told the officer the truth about who I was.

Holly raises her eyebrows.

'So, you had no idea who she was, or that she was linked to that lot?'

'None. This wasn't planned. I don't know what made me stop, as I'm not one for getting involved in other people's misery. I know what it is to be desperate, though. Maybe that was enough.'

'Let's hope it leads to something positive with this lot. It's the closest I've got to one of the targets. With any luck, they'll be back,' Holly says, in a warmer tone.

I agree. Job well done, I'd say.

8

Vince called the next morning. He wanted a meeting at the Flying Squad office. It's a portacabin in the car park at the old Hendon training school. There are very few police buildings left. Remote working is the preferred order of the day.

I love remote working. It means I can be where I need to be, doing what I need to do, when I need to do it. After that, there's time for police work. I don't really regard myself as a criminal, more a disgruntled public servant who seeks justice and administers it directly.

I'll always support the victim. Always. Like the girl on the bridge. She didn't deserve to die. Motormouth outside the pub? That's what I call karma. Vince is ready to start the meeting. Myself, Holly, and Winter are present.

'I've had intel look at the footage from the covert cameras yesterday. Sugar was the driver. Hopefully, he'll return with Nines, and Toots. The news on the other two is helpful too. Bigga and Cheeko are their street names. Bigga is the guy doing all the chat and Cheeko is his cohort. Both are involved in drugs and guns. They are enforcers for a gang on the estate called The Blood Shedderz.' Vince flicks through his notes then closes the file.

Meeting over. My departure is interrupted by Winter.

'Batford, I need a word before you go,' she says.

The room clears.

'I've seen the CCTV footage. You acted with restraint, and I was pleased to see it. I hope this will continue. I want names on charge sheets, not bodies in bags. The commissioner has requested regular updates on this operation.'

I motion to speak, but she puts up her hand.

'Consider this a heads-up, Sam. It seems we're both subject to a level of monitoring neither of us desire. Let me down, and you'll be looking for another job,' she says, cramming papers into an oversized shoulder bag.

I wish I had her dedication to the service.

'Thanks for the shit sandwich, ma'am. I'll be off.' I make for the door behind her.

She blocks my path.

'I won't forget the previous operations we were involved in. The evidence that didn't arrive where it should have. Wrap the shit sandwich for later or swallow it. Your call.' With that, she strides towards the meeting-room door and leaves. The scent of her perfume hangs in the air.

Within seconds, Vince returns from the main office.

'I overheard what she said. The walls are thin. Man, she hates you. It's not like the good old days when you never saw a senior officer unless you were in the shit. We're all accountable now, Sam,' he says, looking serious. 'Like Winter, I need this job to come off too. I'm looking at a promotion to DCI. Help me with that. If she shafts you, I'll see you right with me.' As he says this, he is nodding like an annoying toy dog.

I step closer and push my shoulders back. We're nose-to-nose.

'I'll do what I'm tasked with doing, and I'll manage my own career path, guv.'

I'm done with overbearing supervision. I brush past Vince and leave.

9

Holly stayed at Hendon to catch up on paperwork. The garage is locked with a "Back Soon" sign taped to the door. I'm sitting in the living room of my estate flat, deciding on my next move. If the landing patrol knew me, they'd realise we're not dissimilar in our feelings of hostility towards authority.

A sound of splintering wood crashes into my thoughts. Someone's forcing entry to the flat. The pane in the front door shatters, followed by a cracking of wood as something heavy hits the door frame. I get up and contemplate fleeing out of the lounge window. I try the window. It doesn't open fully – a design to stop people falling out. It would be too high, anyway. Whoever's entering has no intention in having a quiet chat. I have one option – to fight.

There's a final crash. Unknown voices enter my domain. There are no shouts of "Police". This is no raid. It's the other enemy.

I move behind the lounge door.

I recognise one of the voices as Bigga, the mouthy one in the garage and defender of the landing. Bigga enters the lounge carrying a short-handled axe. I waste no time in introducing him to a baseball bat I'd brought from the safe house in Scotland. I swing it towards him.

The tip of the hickory connects with his jaw, and he reels back into Cheeko. I send the bat crashing between Bigga's shoulder blades. The axe drops to the floor. Cheeko whips out a blade, flailing it around. He's unable to step over Bigga who's face down and not moving.

'Have you not heard of knocking?' I say.

Cheeko isn't amused. 'You dumb fuck, you're a dead man,' he says, then lunges with the blade.

Using an underhand swing, the tip of the bat connects with his lower jaw. The bat follows through, ready for strike two. Cheeko's face makes contact with the wood. I clock his eyes as he tastes blood. His face contorts with rage.

I strike again. The bat hits Cheeko's shoulder, and he joins Bigga on the floor. Sugar is at the door. He looks at the carnage and hesitates. His cohorts lie on the floor, moaning. Blood seeps from cuts to their faces. Sugar looks at his mates and back at me.

'Wait!' I shout. 'I don't want any more of this. Tell me what you want. This isn't the way I conduct business. I thought you heard my boss's offer.'

Sugar steps back.

I lower the bat off my shoulder and open my left hand, showing it's empty.

'I'm here because it's better than being homeless. I never asked for this shit. I'm an ex-soldier trying to make a living. I swear that I never knew that girl on the bridge and wish I'd never fucking stopped now.'

Sugar's shoulders relax. I mirror him. Bigga and Cheeko remain where they are, moaning.

'Why don't we start again?' I say. 'I'm Sky.' I dropped the ex-soldier in early. Hopefully, he'll think I'm good around guns and vehicles. That I could be of further use to them. If not, at least it might explain my instinct for self-preservation.

Sugar eyes me cautiously. 'Your boss said the BMW needs work doing. You weren't at the garage. "Back Soon" means five minutes, not five hours. I thought you were ignoring us, so we came to you.'

I step aside, inviting Sugar to step over his mates. He accepts and comes into the lounge. My impression of him is that he'll have control over the two on the floor if they act up.

Sugar stands near the window. Bigga and Cheeko sit on the floor, wiping blood from their mouths. Bigga looks at Sugar. Sugar motions with a downward palm to stay where he is.

I need to gain control of the situation now.

'If we're to talk, it's on my terms,' I say. 'I don't trust anyone. Phones on the floor, batteries out. Any other weapons, do the same.'

Bigga and Cheeko look at Sugar. Sugar places two phones on the window ledge. He breaks the back to an old Nokia and drops the battery. That's his dirty line.

He shuts down an iPhone and places it on the table in front of him. He places a car key next to the phones on the windowsill.

Bigga and Cheeko have the same phone set-up as Sugar. Cheeko produces two blades. One is a butterfly knife he had strapped to his ankle. They place them all at their feet. All seems calm now.

I address Sugar.

'So, do you want some work doing on the BMW beyond the exhaust? Service, MOT?' I stick with legit stuff, but I know the way they entered was for effect. They want more than what was offered at the garage. I'm not wearing a wire, but there's a portable recording device in the room that's voice activated.

Sugar speaks for the group. 'We ain't discussing nothing till we know more about you. Word on the street is that your boss ain't all that. It all looks suss. That garage has been shut for months. The last owner didn't listen to what we wanted and was moved on. Now you come along ripping up the neighbourhood and fucking people off with your attitude. Something ain't right.'

Sugar leans against the windowsill, arms across his chest. Bigga and Cheeko lean forward.

'I went to her looking for work. I did a bit of mechanics in the army, so she took me on. I saw it as a way off the street. Council housed me through a veterans' charity,' I say.

'What regiment were you in?' Bigga says.

'That's my business. The army taught me to kill and avoid being killed. That's all you need to know. You lot don't look like you could afford a Beamer of that quality, so maybe I should be the one wanting to know more about you before I say yes to working with you.'

They look at each other and Sugar starts laughing.

'Like you, our business is need-to-know. You can handle yourself, and it's good you know mechanics. Welding is what we need. The car's good, engine-wise, but luggage space is tight. Would be good to increase it, you know what I'm saying?' Sugar says.

'Nowhere to store your lunch, that kind of thing,' I say. 'I find door spaces useful. Floors and boots too.'

'Now we're talking. We carry the kind of tools that don't get left in the vehicle overnight. You'll know all about those,' Cheeko says.

Sugar shoots him a glance. He's spoken out of line.

I jump on it.

'I hear you. I used to carry those tools too. I can help, but I'll need dimensions. I work from sight. No guessed measures. The money will need to be good too.'

Sugar steps towards me and leans in. 'I'll be in touch. Sorry about your door.' He gestures to the others to get up and leave.

No numbers exchanged, but I sense they'll be back. These guys aren't the type to make appointments. The garage will have to open later or at least give the appearance it's available to passing trade.

I message Vince and Holly. The flat's too open to talk on the phone. Vince will organise the new flat door.

I grab my holdall. I'm not staying in insecure premises. I stood outside them enough in my probation. Time has come to show the estate I've nothing to hide. Should they wish, they can look inside. There's nothing worth stealing.

The envelope from Yvonne stares back from the top of my grab bag. Seems like an ideal time to check out my inheritance. I pick up my phones, collect the keys to the Mini, and leave. No requirement to close anything behind me. Such is my world. One open door.

* * *

DI Vince Gladwell waits in the office of Winter's personal assistant while Winter is on the phone. The PA's phone rings. A brief one-sided conversation takes place and Vince is invited into Winter's office. He sits opposite her.

'Thanks for agreeing to see me, ma'am. I was in the building and thought it would be easier to come to you than call,' Vince says, balancing an A4-size blue book on his knee.

'I have a couple of minutes, so fire away,' Winter says.

'I'll be as quick as I can. Our subject, Sugar, has engaged with Batford and asked him to create space for "tools" in what we believe is the BMW. The meeting was covertly recorded. They forced entry to Batford's flat. I have to say, Batford showed significant restraint. Bigga and Cheeko were present.'

'What does "significant restraint" mean to you?'

'From what I could see from the covert footage, Bigga and Cheeko have suffered facial injuries and there's nothing left of the front door to the flat. I'm planning to have the flat secured. DS Batford is away from the premises until it's deemed fit for him to return.'

Winter makes notes and looks across at Vince.

'Reasonable force?'

'I'd say so. They entered with an axe and Batford used a baseball bat in self-defence.'

'Well, looks like we're up and running.'

'It certainly does. I know your feelings about Sam, ma'am, but he does get the job done.'

Winter inhales deeply.

'I know Sam of old, ma'am. He won't mess me about. If he does, I'll take him down along with the gang,' Vince says.

Winter stands and holds out her hand across the desk.
'On that note, keep up the great work,' she says.
Vince shakes her hand and leaves.

10

I don't use GPS or a sat nav. Like a slug, they leave a trace. It's an *A-Z* of London for me. The address I need is in East London. A strange area for Mike to have a property. I arrive at the security gates of a small industrial site. In the envelope is an access card. A four-digit code on a Post-it is attached to it. I lean out of the car window and place it in a slot at the gate. There's a click and the gates open. I drive in. The gates close behind me. There are no obvious cameras, but I sense I'm being observed.

I locate the commercial unit that's shown on the papers and drive past. A shuttered double garage door is down. There are no lights coming from under the steel. I park the Mini, get out, and walk back to the unit. No one has followed me. The area's deserted. This is one huge storage site.

There's a code entry system on the wall to the right of the up-and-over reinforced steel doors. I tap in the numbers I'd remembered from the note. To the left of the code box is a standard entrance door. It's reinforced. The lock clicks. I push the door. Lights come on as I step inside, and the door self-closes.

The floor space is large enough to house a small fleet of vehicles and there are four covered over at the far end. It feels strange being here with Mike in my holdall. I place my bag on a lounge chair. The seat is one of three leather tub chairs grouped around an Ercol coffee table. There's a bar with a set of optics. A projector sits on a marble bar top. There's another Post-it on a bottle of whisky in the optics, which reads:

> Grab a drink, you're going to need it. Sit
> down and press play.

There's a remote on the bar. This is too surreal. My heart rate increases as my eyes take it all in. It feels like I've walked into a chic, industrial loft living space but on ground level. An elite city dweller lad's pad or car showroom. I can't place it.

As I take in my environment, I notice an internal office pod building. I take a crystal tumbler, fill up a measure from the bottle of whisky the note was attached to, and sit in the chair. My fingers stroke the remote and I press play.

The white wall of the pod becomes Mike's face. He filmed it here as the covered cars are in the background. He was sitting in the seat I'm in and it looks like he was using the glass I'm drinking from. I've only seen one glass. I'm assuming he didn't receive guests.

He raises his glass to me. I look at the box I've placed on the table. His voice leaks out of the projector speakers.

'All right, my son, if you're watching this, I'm either lying low abroad or dead. Either way, you're here because of Yvonne.'

'This is yours now. My little bolthole for whenever the heat got too much at home or work. Do with it all as you wish. Yvonne would have told you it was a different type of property you'd inherited. There's another. I'll get to that.'

He shifts his position to the edge of the chair, leaning into the camera. This was made recently. The shirt and tie combo matches what he was wearing when he shot himself.

'The area's sound. Like-minded businesspeople operate from this site. One thing's imperative. You never bring anyone here, ever. It's a rule on purchase. Don't breach it. You'll have seen a small pod. You can live and sleep there should you need to. There's a secure line managed by a private firm. All internet is accessed through that.' He sits back and sips his drink.

'I've paid up front for the unit and all resources. Everything's managed through a private company, so you'll be getting no bother at all. The site is under constant watch. The control centre has your image. That's why you've got this far. They won't call our lot. They have their own security team – ex-soldiers, most of them special forces. It's as safe as you can get. The inside has been swept for sight and sound. It's clean.'

He pauses to take another drink, then continues.

'I purchased another place in London. Where we used to meet, Thameside, is either in the hands of the police or they haven't linked me to it yet. In the pod is an address for your new accommodation. It's in a name you'll have all the documentation for. My parting gift. I wasn't just working with you, Sam. I never told you everything. It was to protect myself. Not that I didn't trust you, I did. It got out of control though, even for me. It's no good to me now, and I'll be fucked if I'm letting Yvonne have a penny more than she has. She's not stupid, Sam. She needed looking after to keep her quiet. It's up to you whether you carry on as we were or decide to go straight now that I'm gone. Good luck, mate. Dead or alive, you'll never hear from me again.' He raises his glass, and the recording terminates.

He had it all planned. He was on his toes with Razor. My guess is he thought Winter would bang me up and I'd say nothing and take the fall for us both. He underestimated me and paid the price. He was confident no one else would be viewing this, or he wouldn't have named me in the recording. I find the external playing device with the USB stick and eject it for destruction. So, all this is mine, I can do with it what I wish. He'd obviously invested better than he let on. He clearly had many decent jobs rolling at once that didn't include me. I feel used.

Maybe the work he involved me in was just for his kicks or to put the scent on me while other jobs he had running couldn't be covered by police. Resources are limited. He had knowledge of all the operations that were using covert assets.

I take my drink and go the pod. There's another code entry system. I use the same four digits. The door to the pod slides back into an internal frame. The pod is the length of a standard static home on a caravan site. It's cleanly decorated. There's a bedroom with a super king bed, en suite, and a full kitchen. At the back is a door that's shut. I enter. It's an office, all hooked up with a computer and a phone. He's left a picture of himself grinning inanely to the camera.

He's left his police-issue laptop. I turn the picture frame face-down; I've seen enough of him today. He did well. This is like a fortress. On the back of the picture frame is an inscription in his writing.

Turn me back the right way, you bastard.

I smile and stand it up again.

I check the desk drawers. They're empty. A single picture of the Met Police crest adorns the wall. Moving it from the wall reveals a safe. I enter the same code and it opens. Inside is a leather man-bag, which I take out, and open. There's a passport, driving licence, and birth certificate for a Peter Ripley. I open the passport and see my image, same on the driver's licence. Good to know I'll have the means to disappear if I need to.

There's a door key and the address for a residential premises. The deeds for a flat are all there. The bag still feels heavy. I remove what looks like twenty grand in cash and see the outline of the handle of a gun wrapped in an oil-soaked rag. I unwrap the weapon. It's a SIG-Sauer P228, 9mm, semi-automatic with two clips, both full. The gun looks new. I wrap it back in the rag and place it in the bag it came from. There's comfort in knowing I have access to it. As a rule, I don't carry. The memory of the day I was shot returns and I shake my head to get rid of it. My prosthetic lower left leg is the only reminder I can't dispose of. I check my watch. I need to meet Vince and Holly.

A visit to my new residential property can wait for another day. I need to be back at the estate flat tonight. I don't check the cars either. My brain is still processing what Mike's left me. I'm struggling to take it all in.

On meeting him, you'd never have guessed he was so resourceful. I take my bag, leaving Mike on the table. He'll be safer here than with me. I kill the lights and head for the Mini and central London.

11

I leave the Mini in a parking facility in Bloomsbury Square Garden and walk to High Holborn. Holborn is busy with tourists and city workers. I take a back road towards the British Museum and enter a park area near it. I need to be certain Winter and Vince aren't having me followed. Especially after visiting my inheritance. The likes of Sugar don't concern me.

I sit on a bench and massage my left thigh. The limb feels fatigued. I'm not alone. A vagrant occupies the other end of the seat. People drift past – mothers with prams, joggers, and lovers. The sun is out. The open space is bathed in warmth. The vagrant must be uncomfortable carrying the multiple layers he's wearing. He's not on surveillance; dirty hair, a look of desperation and despair, along with the smell of an unwashed body tell me this.

The obvious points that a surveillance team would use are empty. The vagrant's eyes catch mine. He awkwardly gets up to leave. I place my hand on his arm and gently ease him back to stay seated. His arm trembles.

'I'm going soon – you stay,' I say.

As he leans forward to stand up, his coat opens at the chest. Attached to his next layer of clothing is a run of staggered medals. He clocks I've noticed them and pulls his coat across his body.

'Relax, I'm taking five minutes while I wait for some mates. I used to be in the army. Where did you get the medals?'

His lips press together in a slight grimace. His eyes become watery.

He looks around before undoing his jacket and turning the medals towards me. Each medal is anchored to his shirt by safety pins. I recognise campaign medals for Iraq and Afghanistan. The one that grabs my attention is a Military Cross. As I register the medal, my chest tightens, accompanied by an overwhelming need to swallow. He turns away and sits back against the bench.

'I miss my mates,' I say. 'I bet you do too. I guess we're lucky enough to be here, on the same bench, enjoying the sun.'

I reach into my bag and bring out a bundle of notes. 'Here, take this. You need it more than me.'

He ignores my gesture and gets up to leave, adjusting a green bungee cord that holds a pair of decaying waterproof trousers round his sunken waist. He grabs the handle of a trolley that contains all he owns and walks away.

I look at the wodge of notes, open the bag, and shove the notes in. Despite the fella's appearance, I'm the one feeling unclean. It was crass, offering a man of honour dirty money. Look where the money's got me.

My work phone beeps. It's Vince on WhatsApp.

In the area, be there in five.

The soldier's gone. I cross Great Russell Street, keeping the British Museum behind me, then head into Bury Place, taking a left into Pied Bull Yard. There was a direct route across the park, but I needed to get my head back in the game. An anti-surveillance pattern works every time for me.

Vince, Holly, and Winter are already in the pub. I go to the bar, get a drink, and head towards the table they're at. To my surprise, they've dressed appropriately for the setting. No suits. Winter has chosen skinny jeans that fit her well, along with an AC/DC tour T-shirt and a pair of Converse. I had her down as a classical girl with a penchant for boy bands.

Holly and Vince are casually dressed too. Vince gives up his seat. He knows I won't relax unless I have line of sight on the pub's door. I sit down and Winter kicks things off.

'I appreciate this isn't the best of venues for a covert team to meet with their operational leads, but money for meeting rooms is tight. Meeting outdoors keeps us on our toes. Keeps our tradecraft fresh. I've had word your flat door's been boarded up, Sam. A new door is on order. Here are the keys for the lock on the temporary replacement.'

I take the keys and Winter hands over to Vince.

'I've reviewed the covert camera footage from inside your flat. You did well. It won't see court, don't worry,' he says.

'I'm not concerned. What about you, Klara?' I say.

Winter looks my way. 'This is Vince's job. I've authorised the removal of the recording equipment and that's been done. Couldn't risk its discovery when the flat was not secured. I appreciate the equipment was concealed, but you weren't there so I felt it prudent to make certain the flat was clean in case they returned for a closer inspection. The main thing is that contact has been established, which was a crucial aim in the operation. Do you need anything else for the garage?' Winter looks to Holly.

'We'll need cutting and welding equipment. We must appear like we are doing the work,' Holly says, looking at me.

I agree.

'I'll get that arranged,' Vince says.

'My team are primed and ready to roll. They'll be working lates and nights due to the targets' lifestyles. If you are with the targets, be aware my lot could be close. Your backup is unaffected,' Vince says.

'You mean our backup remains non-existent,' Holly says.

'No. I'll be there as quick as I can.' Vince's shoulders shift as he laughs.

He knows the score as well as we do. We're on our own. Don't do anything stupid.

Vince checks his watch. 'I appreciate this could have been covered by phone, but Klara and I wanted to meet you to make sure you feel supported. That said, I need to leave now,' he says.

'Me too. I've plenty to get on with,' Holly says.

'Be at the garage tomorrow unless either of you get contacted tonight,' Vince says. He and Holly leave together.

Winter downs the remains of her drink. 'I'm getting another. Do you want a top-up?' she says.

'Why not? I'll get them,' I say. I go to the bar and order. I'm conscious of my bag being on the seat next to her.

She'd die if she knew there were thousands of pounds of laundered money in it. I glance back. She's taking a call. I return as she puts her phone down.

'Another operation on the go?' I say, passing her a drink.

'My daughter, checking in,' she says.

46

I choose to deflect from asking about her personal life. Last thing I need is to have to reciprocate in that department.

'How are you finding your new empire?' I say.

She eyes me over her glass, lowering it before she replies.

'Second rate. The National Crime Agency was awash with resources and money. It made work easier. Here, you're begging for staff and cash just to stay afloat. Anyway, I appreciate this is probably as awkward for you as it is for me, but if our working relationship is to be fruitful, we must move forward, so what's your tactical plan for this job? I noticed you acquiesced to Holly about garage resources, which is most unlike you.'

I drape my arms over the back of my chair. 'My plan, Klara, is to do as I'm told.' I give her a wry smile.

She purses her lips.

'Very funny,' she says.

She retrieves a packet of Rothmans from her handbag and picks up her drink. 'I need a cigarette. Let's go outside,' she says, giving me no choice in the matter.

I take my drink and follow her into a courtyard. We sit at a rustic metal table. She offers me a cigarette and I accept.

'How have you been since Mike's funeral?' she says, sitting back, crossing her legs.

This feels too intimate. I know her operationally, but not personally. As with any enemy, I like to keep them close until the day of disposal. I light my cigarette from hers and enjoy the first intake of nicotine. Dappled light catches her blonde highlights.

I retrieve a pair of shades from my bag. I don't want her reading my eyes. For a moment, it's as though we're two people out in London with nothing more to do than relax. No stress, no pressure, no responsibilities. I'm considering a response when the sound of an explosion shatters the illusion. A sound like the explosion of the van doors outside Sainsbury's.

People are running into shops, in a state of confusion. I need to move us to an open space. This is the kind of place they'd run to if the job went wrong.

'On my say, we run for the exit that leads to the park, ready?'

Winter nods.

'Now,' I say.

We get up from a crouch and move.

We stop momentarily as we exit the courtyard. Sirens are blaring. People are walking around in a daze, trying to work out where the commotion is coming from. Phones move in circles in the hope of catching something. My hearing's alerted to the high revs of an engine. As quickly as it registers, the car swings into view.

The rear of a BMW fishtails before the tyres grip the road. It's Sugar's BMW. I grab Winter, leaning into her neck as the car approaches. The car speeds past us, towards Holborn. I release Winter and we separate.

'It was them, wasn't it?' Winter says, looking at the road the BMW left along.

'Yeah, it was them. Thankfully, they were focused on getting away. I must get to the garage. They may go there,' I say.

Winter's phone rings. She answers it.

'Winter.' She mouths "Vince" to me. I wait while she takes the call. This all felt too close for comfort.

'...I'll tell Sam, he's here, too. Contact Holly, tell her to join Sam. I'm heading back to New Scotland Yard,' she says, terminating the call.

'Surveillance lost them before the hit. Vince is fuming. Contact me if you need anything,' she says. With that she heads towards High Holborn tube station, ponytail in full sway as she strides towards a cabstand.

I need to be away before police start locking down the area. The show's over. Normality resumes.

Sensitive log entry 26

Today was a disaster. By arranging an open meeting, I'd hoped to convey a relaxed atmosphere where Batford and I would engage socially. DI Gladwell played his part by making excuses to leave, and DC Burns followed.

It was my intention to have an icebreaker with Batford. Organising an operational meeting meant he'd turn up. I needed to gain a sense of trust.

My trust-building was thwarted by an armed robbery involving our subjects. They used an explosive to gain entry into a security van.

I must assess the risk to the public against the risk to all officers involved in the operation. I'll ask for more outside resources to provide armed cover. Whether they can be deployed is debatable.

I hope it's all worth it in the end. It would be nice to have some family time soon. These hours are killing me.

Entry complete.

Klara Winter – Detective Superintendent
Covert Policing
Authorising Officer
Op Envy

12

LBC radio has the robbery as its lead news item, everyone's raising the question of why it took so long for the police to arrive. The bulletin ends with the publication of new statistics showing a steep rise in violent crime.

I switch over to BBC 6 Radio Music. My phone goes. It's Holly.

'Where are you? We've got customers,' she says.

Just as I suspected, they've arrived.

'I'm five minutes out,' I say, and kill the line.

Ignoring the speed limit, the five minutes become three. I swing the Mini onto the forecourt to the garage. The main doors are open.

Sugar and two others with their backs to me are sitting on the ramp. There's no sign of the BMW. I drive straight in, making them shift rapidly as my tyres hit the steel platforms of the ramp, gliding to a stop at the end. I exit quickly, saying nothing, pressing the button that brings the main door down.

'Sorry I'm late. I got held up,' I say to Holly.

'Not good enough. Speak to this lot, and what's with the main door going down?' she asks.

Not the question I'd expect when I'm trying to create an illusion of privacy.

'I passed a police car. Thought they might tail me. I didn't think you'd appreciate them coming here.'

Holly nods. The penny's dropped that Vince's team is out.

'Get the kettle on. Mine's a tea, milk three lumps and whatever they want,' Holly says, affirming her role as boss, while she resumes her inspection of an engine suspended on a pulley. "They" meaning Sugar and his comrades:

Nines and Toots. I recognise them from the still from the surveillance camera.

They're shifty; their eyes darting about, hands in and out of pockets. I'd feel the same after the job they've just pulled off. They follow me into the kitchen leaving Kat with the engine. I grab a whisky bottle from under the sink and the required mugs. No tea or coffee for this lot.

I pour good measures and indicate they take them as I whack tea bags in two mugs and fill the kettle. I down my shot. The warmth feels good. Relaxes me before business begins.

I wait for one of them to say why they're here. All good for the garage cameras. Nines is the first to speak.

'My man, Sugar, says you can help us out with a bit of work.'

'That depends on what you want doing,' I say. 'I'm just a mechanic, as I repeatedly told him.'

Nines smiles and the other two relax as the whisky takes effect.

Then he strolls over to a stool and perches on the edge. 'Mechanics is what I need', he says. 'The kind of mechanic I'm seeking must be good with his hands as well as tools, ya get me?'

I nod.

He continues, 'Sugar says you were army? So, you'll know how to take direction and what can happen if you don't. He told me you deliver a good kicking if people step out of line. They were my soldiers you beat on. That wasn't a clever move.'

I've heard enough. I try to remember my role here, but the soldier in me is screaming not to take this shit on my own turf. Yes, I'm undercover, but this guy's taking a huge liberty thinking he can stroll onto my ground and tell me that if I don't do what he asks, then I'm done for. So I address his concerns.

'Nice speech. You don't know anything about me or what I'm capable of. The fools you sent to deliver a message got off lightly. I don't know you either, but I've let you enter my place of work without an appointment, drink my whisky, and speak freely. Let's start again. Threats don't work with me.'

Toots is riled. He's breathing like a police horse before a baton charge. Nines remains cool.

'I like you,' Nines says. 'I sent them round your place. I needed to see if you were a player or a patsy. I don't make a habit of meeting those I don't need to. I'm sure you understand where I'm coming from.'

I observe Nines over the lip of my mug.

He continues his sermon. 'Your boss said the BMW needed some work. That motor has served its time. We need another. The motor will need some modifications doing for our line of business. Now, as the good mechanic you are, can you sort us a car?'

'For the right money, I can find you a car and dispose of the BMW too. From what you're saying, it sounds like it shouldn't be on the street,' I say, raising my eyebrows.

The car would be great evidence and I've been told by Vince that evidence is what he needs.

Nines gestures to Toots, who reaches behind his back. I grab a long-handled wrench that was under the worktop next to me and raise it to throw at his head. Sugar steps in front.

'Whoa, he's going for the dough. He ain't strapping.' I look to Nines who raises his palms towards me in a gesture that says calm down. I lower the wrench. Toots produces a roll of notes and hands them to Nines.

'There's enough to cover your expenses. How you get us a car, I'll leave with you. It can't be hot. Make sure of that. If this works out, there'll be more where this comes from.' Nines throws me the roll and I catch it. It's weighty, which helps.

I nod. 'I appreciate your faith. The boss won't ask questions. I'll pay her a percentage of my take on this one. How will I get hold of you?'

Nines sees a notepad and pencil on the counter. He writes down a number and passes it to me.

'Get me on this line. Don't fuck me about. Fail, and I'll want that cash back with interest added.'

'Here's my number, so you know it's me when I call,' I say, handing him a written note.

'Where's the BMW you need rid of?' I ask.

'Sugar will bring it. What's your name?' Nines asks.

'Sky.'

'I'm Nines, this is Toots. I know you and Sugar have been introduced. Good doing business,' Nines says.

'Don't go out the front. Use this fire exit,' I say to them. I press the exit bar and look out. There's no one about. They leave separately. Nines is the last one to go. He comes close and puts his arms out to hug. This isn't a sign of affection – he's making certain I'm not wired, something he should have done before he spoke. I let him conduct his hug down and he leaves happy I'm clean.

'How'd it go? You were in there a while,' she says as I enter the work area of the garage.

I show Holly the roll of notes, phone number, and explain the conversation. She's overjoyed it's finally playing out.

I return to the kitchen area, grab a chair, and retrieve an evidence bag from a concealed space in a false air vent. I bag and seal the money, then separately bag and seal the pad the number was written on. One of Vince's detectives will covertly enter the garage and collect the three exhibits.

I step outside, needing a smoke, and to knock back some morphine as the leg's playing up. Phantom pain, my consultant calls it. I sit on a pile of tyres and light up.

Holly soon joins me.

'We need new cars,' she says, sitting beside me. 'The ones we have that look like they're being worked on have been seen by them now. If this garage was for real, they'd be gone by the next time they come around.'

'I'll get Vince on it. We need a vehicle for this lot too and Vince can get it wired up. He can drop them all off here as one lot,' I say.

I lie back on the tyres. The heat of the sun on the rubber provides welcome warmth for my back. The swinging of that baseball bat must have jarred my shoulder muscles.

'What got you into this game?' Holly says inquisitively.

'Mike recruited me when he took over in covert policing. He said I'd be good at this type of work. Told me he needed a decent DS on board as the last one was retiring. How about you?'

'I always wanted to do it, I guess. Manchester was always on the lookout for females. I fitted the bill. Problem is, I'm borrowed by other forces all the time. A lack of female UCs, hence me being back here so quick,' she says, swatting a fly away.

She gets up as a BMW approaches. They were quick.

The front end is smashed. It's a miracle it's still driveable. They must have had a prang after we saw them. Sugar limps the car into the garage and kills the engine. He gets out and throws me the keys.

'Get rid of it. Let us know when you've sorted another,' Sugar says, initiating a fist bump. I reciprocate, and with formalities done, Sugar walks off. Holly waits until he's out of sight before she speaks.

'Like to see how you're going to get the BMW in the roof space?' She laughs, pointing to the car. She gets out her phone and dials.

'Vince? It's Holly. The package is here and needs lifting. Bring a couple more for show.' She listens for a couple of beats and finishes the call.

She turns to me. 'Vince will arrange everything. He has transport and drivers for covert collections. They'll get it away later today to be forensically examined and stored. I'll manage that. Until then, I'm shutting shop to avoid any further contamination. At least the inside of the car is as secure as he left it. It's all looking good.' She wipes her brow, leaving a light oil streak on her tanned forehead.

I don't point it out.

'Vince won't stop just because we have the car,' I say. 'He'll want them taken out doing a job to maximise the chances of prosecution. We know they aren't looking to stop. We need them doing proper time. I'll be off. I have other business to take care of. Bell me if you need me.' I get ready to leave.

'Anything interesting?' Holly asks.

'Personal stuff,' I say.

She accepts my reply and probes no more.

* * *

My return to the estate flat doesn't go unnoticed. The estate's neighbourhood watch scheme is out in force.

I move along the landing towards the large wooden panel that is now my front door. I unlock the heavy-duty steel lock and enter the flat. The wood shuts and seals better than the old door ever did. Extra bolts have been installed internally, which I'm grateful for.

The baseball bat's where I left it. The rest of the flat's untouched too. This operation is unnerving me. It's going too smoothly for my liking. For once, I'm in a position of playing the police game and assisting an investigation rather than playing my own game and disrupting one. This group is different, though.

They're risk takers. They're not put off by the last job.

I can hear female voices, giggling and laughing, on the landing – Eastern European accents. There are men's voices too, but these sound like they're Russian. Then, there's a sound of high-heels on concrete.

I have my ear to the rough grain of the flat door, mindful I may get another visitor. I can hear raised voices between a man and one of the girls followed by the distinctive sound of a slap on skin.

Next door's flat door might be open. There's a scuffle then the sound of a door shutting.

I need to show the estate I'm going nowhere. It will affirm to Nines I'm a man of action. Nines has shown how he chooses to operate. Now I need to demonstrate my resourcefulness.

13

The neighbours continued to party last night. The sounds through the thin flat walls were enough to make me go to the industrial site. I took the opportunity to inspect the vehicles Mike had bought. A Tesla Model 3 was his only attempt to reduce his carbon footprint. A charging point in the unit ensured the car was fully juiced. A Porsche 911, Jaguar F-Type coupe, and an Audi R8 V10 Plus completed the set. None float my boat.

None of the cars appear to have been used. It's as if he just wanted to waste money or get rid of it fast. Time for me to get to the garage.

* * *

The BMW was lifted last night and the exhibits extracted from the false air vent in the kitchen. The recovery unit deposited two cars for us to appear to be working on. The garage doors are down as we prep for the day ahead.

A loud bashing on the metal doors interrupts me. I leave via the fire exit off the kitchen. Holly remains inside. Inching around the wall, I listen for sounds of conversation, for any indication of whether the person is alone or not. It's 8 a.m. I'm not expecting any of that crew to be up, let alone out.

I reach the corner of the garage and pause. The bashing sounds again, louder. The metal rattler steps back and into my line of sight. It's Nines.

I step towards him. 'We're not open.'

Nines darts a look in my direction and reaches behind him, then stops. 'What are you doing creeping up on a guy like that? Why didn't you rack the door up, for fuck's sake?'

It's clearly too early for him.

'Like I said, we're shut. I wasn't expecting you back so soon. You should have called first.'

'We need to talk,' he says.

I need to hear what he wants out of earshot of Holly and the covert mic and camera. 'Let's hit the tyres,' I say, chinning the air towards the makeshift rubber seating.

'Do I look like I want to get grease and shit on these threads?'

He's dressed in what could only be described as smart street casual; smart enough to impress without looking like you're dressed for court. I wonder if he hasn't been home since yesterday.

'I'll sit – you talk. I'll be on my feet all day while you're sleeping off your all-nighter,' I say.

Nines smirks. 'You're a shrewd guy for a mechanic. There's something not right about you, but I'm cool though. True, I was out last night with the fellas at a casino up west. I was hoping I could get rid of some of the dough we had lying about by playing the tables. Didn't go as well as we expected, but fuck it, we're here for a good time, not a long time.' He takes out a spliff and sparks up.

'How much are you down?' I say.

'None of your concern. Let's say it's more than you'll have ever seen. Thing is, we need that new set of wheels quicker than we thought. You got shot of the Beamer?'

'If you're after that, you're too late. It's been crushed.'

Nines takes a draw and exhales the smoke. The sweet smell invades my synapses. I try to inhale the smoke as it drifts towards me.

A youth on a pushbike idles by. Nines notices the cyclist. He licks his lips and starts pacing towards the road, his hand drifting to the base of his back. The first shot ricochets off the steelwork of the door. I roll off the tyres, palm in the dirt, head slightly raised. Nines ditches the spliff, leaps, and falls down the other side of the tyres.

Holly appears, crouched at the side of the garage, a wheel brace at her feet. Nines is by my side, a 9mm held side on, gangster style. He's shaking. We're all waiting for the next round to fly, but nothing happens. Holly runs over to us. Nines still has the gun locked in his grip. I place my hand on his wrist. He blinks back to the present.

He looks at the gun, then me, places it to the rear of his body, the barrel nestled in his waistband. Holly says nothing. The shooter has left. Sirens invade the still air. A resident has called it in.

I turn to Nines. 'Go.'

Nines doesn't need asking twice. He slinks away, phone to his ear, mouth moving.

'Are you okay?' Holly touches my hand.

I flinch. I'm aware I'm staring at a point in the road. The first car has arrived on the scene, tyres skidding to a halt, doors opening as armed officers deploy. We remain where we are, raise our hands, and place them on our heads.

Two officers approach, weapons drawn, index fingers against the side of the trigger housing. We're frisked by one while the other covers him. Finding we're clean, they relax.

'Put your hands down.' The younger of the two instructs. 'Did you see anything?' he asks.

'I heard what sounded like a car backfiring, then the shutter rattled. We came out to see what was going on then you guys turned up,' Holly says.

The armed officers are joined by regular uniform. I hear the "all clear" over the officer's radio as they approach. I can see one cop has found the point on the door where a bullet must have struck. Police tape is unfurled and looped around. We're now part of a crime scene.

'You may as well pack up for the day. This will take a while to sort out. You'll both have to give your details to one of the plain-clothes guys over there. They'll need to take a statement as to where you were, what you heard, that kind of thing,' the firearms guy says. With that, they leave. Their job is done.

'Best we retreat while we have the chance,' I say to Holly.

As we start to move, a plain-clothes officer approaches. A warrant card hangs on a lanyard round his neck. On the outside of the lanyard are the words "Operation Trident", in bold white letters.

He's carrying an A4-size blue book.

'Who's the owner?' he says, in a broad cockney accent while looking at me.

'I am.' Holly gives him the eye.

'A shot was fired from the street and the bullet went through your garage door. I'll need to speak to you both about what's happened. Are you under any threat at all? Any disgruntled customers that would think to shoot you?' he asks in a nonchalant manner.

'Isn't that for you to establish?' Holly replies. 'As it goes, no, I'm not under any threat.'

The officer shrugs and waves a crime-scene examiner over to photograph the hole in the door.

'I've got to ask,' the officer says. 'We'll need to go inside and see where the bullet ended up. I'll need your contact details and a statement.'

We both give our covert identities as contact details.

Nines is clearly a marked man. We live in a world where no one can be trusted, not even our own. The cyclist must have known Nines was coming and was ready to take a pop. He must have bottled it. Maybe it was a warning shot. The game of survival is stronger than ever at street level. What you have, someone else always wants. There's no sit down and negotiate. Trace and eliminate, the order of the day. Urban warfare, with young foot soldiers willing to please, and babies on the way to take over as they grow up, die, or end up in prison.

We're not allowed inside to gather our belongings. Thankfully, I carry everything I'll need.

My mind's on getting back to the estate and linking with Nines. Holly has other ideas.

'I'll stay and speak to Vince when I can't be overheard. See what he wants from us while this is getting sorted,' she says.

'I'm heading back to the estate. One of the lookouts will tell Nines I'm back. I need to establish where that revolver's being laid down. Do what you need to do here. Vince has my number. He can call me if he needs to.'

I leave and find a bus stop. This job is getting more interesting by the day.

14

I get off a bus and cross the street, choosing a circular route back to the flat. It's a habit I can't shake. The need to be on my guard, alert to conflict, or contact, is ever-present. Even in sleep, my dreams have been dominated by being hunted. Satisfied I'm not being followed, I go to the back of the estate to the alternative entrance to my block.

As I move towards the communal garden below my landing, I look up. A large man is nose-to-nose with a woman. She's crying and looking over the landing wall. I hang back and observe. A neighbour comes out of a flat and tries to placate the guy by putting a hand on his shoulder.

A bad move. The larger male's forehead connects with his nose, and he drops out of view. More men turn up wearing shades and dark T-shirts. The larger male who first appeared with the girl rubs his forehead. His parting gift, a mouthful of phlegm that hits the girl full in the face. She doesn't flinch. She's clearly used to his social etiquette.

The team gets the go-ahead from the leader, and they gradually disperse towards the landing stairs. No sooner are they gone than the usual onlookers re-emerge. I wait a few minutes, then enter the block, happy that the mob will exit at the other end to me. It's not that I don't wish to see them, from an intelligence gathering perspective, it's just that I have other matters requiring my attention. As I reach the landing, a sentry moves towards me, but diverts out of the way. Nines has briefed his staff. My access pass is taken as seen. The girl squats against the landing wall opposite my door. Mascara runs down her cheeks. The cigarette she's lit shakes in her hands. She's in her late teens, but aged by make-up.

My neighbour's door is shut. I find my key. She starts getting up, wincing in pain. She grabs at her abdomen and begins to slump. It's a desperate sight. The skin around her right eye is red and swollen.

'Let me help you. Do you live here?' I ask.

She accepts my help, rising unsteadily to her feet as I support her arm. 'I don't understand much language.' Her accent sounds Eastern European, I think, but I'm no expert. She's still shaking as she props herself against the wall to the flat.

'What happened to you?' I say.

She looks away. 'Nothing. I fell over. That is all.'

As I helped her up, it felt like her muscles surrendered to the extra support. My bet is she's not slept in days.

I can't let her go back in the flat she came from, even if she were welcome. Her cheek is marked by a bruise that looks to be a day old, which corresponds to the slap I heard through my flat wall. I'm surprised she didn't lose teeth.

'Come inside my flat. I'll get you something to drink and eat. You look like shit.'

Tears form. I need to think before I speak.

'You look like you need a rest. Is that better?'

Her lips quiver. I unlock the wooden door panel and I help her in.

I put her on a sofa, and she removes the high-heeled boots she's wearing. I stick the kettle on, leaving her alone in the living room. There's nothing there that will tell her anything about me. She accepts the tea, cradling the mug as she blows across the surface of the drink. Tea, the elixir of life, and universal comforter.

I go to the bedroom and grab a blanket. I'm hoping she doesn't mind prison-cell blue. It's there by design should I ever get asked if I've been nicked. They were so kind. They even let me take the blanket on release, as I had no coat. I hope that part of my legend building won't be required here.

She puts the tea down and accepts the blanket, cocooning herself in the material.

'What's your name?' I say.

Her face peaks out under a hood of blue. 'Olivia. That is the name I was given to say.' She leans forward and takes a sip of tea. Her face flushes with warmth.

'Well, Olivia, it seems you're in a bit of a fix. How'd you get here?'

'Why are you asking? Are you police? Home Office?' She puts the tea down again and curls into a foetal position.

'Do I look like either?' I say, pulling the fabric of my overalls away from my chest.

She smiles. An innocence has returned. Something that was beaten out of her on the landing. I wonder if she's ever felt seen or heard in her life. I know I haven't. Even Mike's display of generosity was motivated by his desire to not let Yvonne get any more than she already had.

'I'm sorry. I'm confused. I have been in your country a month. I was told I'd stay until a work permit is organised. In the meantime, I must do whatever they want me to do.' She looks to the floor.

I've seen suspects do the same before they confess.

'I came to England by boat, in the container of a lorry. I was brought to the flat next to you, with another girl. She is dead… jumped off a bridge…' Her voice fades to a whisper. Her eyes swell with tears and her shoulders convulse as she sobs.

I give her space to release the primal pain before I speak.

I now know the story of the girl on the bridge. Olivia sighs and her breathing regulates.

'How old are you, Olivia?'

She looks up. Her eyes pools of fluid. 'Eighteen,' she says, averting her eyes from mine to the floor.

'Do your family know where you are? Is there anyone you want contacting?' I ask.

She removes the blanket and tries to get up. Her legs are too fatigued to support her. She collapses into the sofa cushion, dragging the blanket around her again.

'If you tell anyone about me, the people next door will kill me and my family back home. Please don't say anything, please, I beg you. I'll do anything you want, no charge, no charge.'

She puts down her tea and collapses into the sofa, surrendering to the will of her body to sleep.

'You're safe with me, Olivia. I won't say anything or ask anything more,' I say. I get up and move the blanket over her shoulders. Her face is turned into the back of the seat.

Great, now I have a victim of people-trafficking asleep on my sofa. I sit down and evaluate what to do next. She can't stay here. The people who've assumed ownership of her will not approve. They'll soon be wondering where she is.

They'll hunt her down and do exactly what they threatened if she can't be found. The gorillas that turned up on the landing had an air of organisation and mindless brutality.

From what I've heard through the walls of our flats, it's clear the enforcers treat Olivia as property to be abused. I remind myself why I'm here. Getting involved in another criminal network's trafficking ring isn't part of the plan.

But I'm not without heart, despite my life choices.

I can't lock her in, but I need to leave. I can't get the police involved. I have my cover to maintain. She'll be seen as a grass, or I will. It wouldn't be a sensible move for either of us. I've had previous dates with death, but death stood me up. I intend to keep it that way.

I take my fleece and grab bag. The landing's clear as I exit left. Leaving the flat unlocked, I make for the stairs, bag in hand. My time here is done. My work phone vibrates in my pocket. It's Vince.

'Where are you? I need to talk.' He sounds reserved, but by his tone, I can tell he wishes to meet sooner rather than later.

I'm at the front of the block now, by the street. I hang back and clock Vince's car. He's taking a risk plotting up here.

He's in the driver's seat, phone to his ear, while he checks himself in the internal mirror.

'I'll see you in two,' I reply, cutting the call.

I exit the block, approaching his car from the rear. He's finished his vanity session deciding to observe the block instead of his pores. Before I enter his car, I pull up the hood on my fleece. As I expected, he hasn't locked the rear doors. With a final scan of the environment, I duck inside the car shutting the door behind me.

'Whoa! What's with sneaking up on me like that? Fuck, I've lost my touch. Should have seen you.' His wide, beaming smile fills the rearview mirror.

I get comfortable and he drives away.

'What's so urgent you had to park outside the block?' I say.

'Welfare check. You were shot at today. I see you have your luggage. What's going on?' he says.

'I'm not staying in that flat. It's not safe. I have somewhere else, don't worry.'

He looks in the rearview mirror again, his brow furrows.

'That's for me to decide, not you. As much as I recognise it's not the most desirable place on the planet, you've been put there for a reason. To make connections with our targets,' he says, returning his focus to the road.

'It's not that simple,' I say.

He beats the steering wheel with his palms. I've hit a nerve.

'Bollocks. There's always an ulterior motive with you. What do you want?' he says.

'That's lovely, that is. You didn't come on a home visit for my welfare. You wanted to make sure I was there. Checking up on me. I'll kip in the garage. It will look good. I'll need a camp bed though, if you could get Winter to open the purse.'

He's having none of it. He pulls the car over in a secluded side street and kills the engine.

He bashes the seat belt release button before launching himself through the gap in the seats. His hands grab my fleece. I break his grip with a twist of my body and step out. Best to take this outside where I can react. I open his door and drag him out the same way he took hold of me, pinning him against the car.

His uppercut connects with my chin, making me bite down on my tongue. I release him as bright flashes fill my head. I feign a left hook while connecting with my right fist into his kidney. He folds like an origami swan. Blood dribbles from my mouth. Vince hands up a Paul Smith floral pocket square. A sign we're done.

I take it and dab my mouth.

'Like old times, eh?' Vince says, sitting on the pavement.

I join him. 'What's with the locker-room antics?' I say.

He wipes his hands on another pocket square.

'Fuck me,' I say. 'How many of those have you got? Are you moonlighting as a magician now that times are tight?'

Vince laughs and places the square away.

'At least my employment would be legal, eh, Sam.' He stares at me, assessing my face for signs of guilt.

'Just because I worked, and associated, with a colleague who turned out to be a villain doesn't mean I'm the same. That's history, Vince. Time to move on. I can't go back to the flat as my neighbours are dodgy and one of them is asleep on my sofa. I want this operation to succeed as much as you and Winter.'

Saying Winter's name in the same sentence as success is not something I thought I'd ever do.

'Mike's dead. I'm here, nursing a bloody mouth you just gave me. I'll say no more of it. I hope you'll do the same. I've got your back, Vince, as I always did.'

With that, he gets up, holds out his hand and pulls me up.

My left stump is throbbing. I need some painkillers. My dirty phone rings. It's Nines. I show Vince the phone and he nods.

'Yo, Sky.' He sounds upbeat. A good sign.

'What's up?' I say.

'Making sure we're still cool after the little thing at the garage earlier?'

'Can't let something like that upset business. I trust you'll deal with it?' I say.

'Yeah, it's all good. I've put the word out. It will be dealt with. I need to see you though, but without your boss woman. It's a bit of work we got, and I need an extra pair of hands.' He pauses.

I look at Vince who can hear the conversation over speakerphone. He shrugs.

'Meet me at the garage, nine o'clock, tonight. She won't be there. Knock on the fire exit,' I say.

'Cool.' He hangs up.

I turn to Vince.

'I'll get my team on him to see what comes of it. Loose follow, don't worry,' Vince says. 'Good call on the garage. That's what I'd come to tell you. The Trident investigation is done. Winter wants an update from me, but I thought I'd see you first.'

'After just now, I wish you'd phoned,' I say, nursing my chin. Vince laughs, and we get back in the car. 'Take me to the nearest tube. I need to clean up. I'll be at the garage an hour before Nines. You can tell Holly. You heard what Nines said. She wouldn't believe me if I told her.'

He drops me at Archway tube station, then leaves. I walk up the hill towards the Whittington Hospital and grab a burger before getting the underground. It's been a tough morning, and it's only midday.

* * *

Back in New Scotland Yard, Vince Gladwell is pacing the PA's office, waiting for Winter to summon him into her domain. He'd contacted her to arrange an update, and she'd made time to accommodate his request. Finally, she phones through to her PA and Vince is shown into her office.

'Thanks for seeing me.' He walks over to a seating area and Winter joins him.

'I'll cut to the chase. The investigation by Trident has concluded, pending any witnesses, or forensic leads. Their SOCO is saying forensic work on the bullet could take weeks. Bottom line, the garage can be reopened. There will be no police visits for the shooting.'

Winter nods her appreciation of the situation. The last thing any of them wants is overt police attention at the garage.

'Are Sam and Holly keeping you updated?' Winter asks.

'I met with Sam after the shooting incident. He's happy to continue in his role. Holly feels the same.'

'So, there's nothing I need to be concerned about at this stage?' Winter says.

Vince shifts in his seat. 'As I've said before, he knows his role as UCO comes under my operational direction. If he screws around, I'll deal with him. I have a dedicated team of detectives who won't tolerate corrupt working practices. He's on the radar and being robustly tracked.'

Winter reflects on his response.

'That's all well and good, Vince, but how well do you know Sam? I've asked around. He's a closed book from what I can gather.'

'I don't see him as corrupt. He's a maverick; volatile and unpredictable, yes, but not bent. Not him. He went a bit cuckoo after getting shot, but who wouldn't? There was a time he confided in me. It was after a drinking session. The team was buzzing at the result of Sam's work. They'd intercepted a significant amount of cocaine, but Sam was in another world. There was no joy about him. He left the pub, and I followed him out. He appeared dissociated, like life had punched all the happiness out of him. I asked him if he was okay. Surprisingly, he admitted he wasn't. Something about the job had triggered a memory. He didn't say what. He did disclose that as a kid, when he showed any excitement at home his foster father would knock it out of him. The guy was a drunk, handy with his fists, and a belt. He lifted his shirt and showed me his back. It was covered in multiple stripes of scar tissue. From what I know of Sam, he wants to see justice done. I've probably said too much.'

Winter rubs her eyes.

'Vince,' she says, 'I appreciate what you've told me, but I'm keeping an open mind. Anything else I need to know?'

'The BMW has been recovered along with the cash Sam was given by Nines. We've traced the notes. They came from a cash-in-transit robbery. Intelligence indicates the gang involved used the same MO and vehicle as our targets. Nines would have to argue he was given the money, and he didn't do the robbery. However, all of this has been obtained using covert tactics. I want them caught in the act, Klara. It's cleaner evidentially.' Vince lets these last words settle with Winter, easing into the seat, waiting for her reply.

'I agree, carry on until you have enough evidence to distance our use of Sam and Holly if it comes to trial.'

Winter stands. Vince leaves the office satisfied all is well in his world.

15

The crime-scene tape has gone. The garage resumes normality. The flip-down numbers of the wall clock states it's 2115 hours. Nines isn't late. He's on street time. A set of car headlights sweeps under the garage. I wait. Two doors close. There's a brief wait before a fist thumps twice against the fire exit door.

'We're closed.'

'It's me, man.'

I recognise Nines' dulcet tones. I push down the locking bar and the door opens. Nines and Sugar enter.

'No Toots?' I say.

'He's sick,' Nines says.

'Okay. So, what's the craic?' I ask. They look at each other. Sugar breaks away and scans the garage.

'Are we alone?' Nines says.

'Yeah, we're alone,' I say.

Both lean against the small kitchen worktop. I grab a bar stool and observe my audience. Nines kicks things off.

'We've got a new job. We want you on board.'

'Depends on the work. I'm busy here,' I say.

'Toots is out. Our schedule don't stop for a sick man. I need a storage facility for some tools, you know what I mean by that?' Nines says.

'Why don't you spell it out? You don't need to fuck about with me. Tell me what you need. I'll consider it,' I say.

Nines strokes his chin.

'The tools I'm talking about come with ammo. I'd need access to them, twenty-four seven, for a runner of mine,' Nines says. He's sitting on the worktop now. A self-appointed king on a makeshift throne.

'Correct me if I'm wrong,' I say. 'You want me to store shooters here, that you, or your runner, can access all day? Fuck me. You don't want much, do you?'

Nines grins. The halogen light reflects a gold tooth that matches his neck chain.

'You're a quick learner. I need to keep our motor here too. The tools of my trade all under one roof. One can't leave without the other. In return, I'll pay your boss a retainer. You'll get a healthy bonus each week, paid in cash, by me. Think of yourself as our operations manager.'

Nines opens his hands like an Italian greeting a relative. It all sounds too good to be true. He's a fool keeping all his eggs in one basket, but that suits me. It could also see this operation put to bed early.

'It isn't my gift to give,' I say.

Both look astonished that I'm batting it off, which I'm not. But as before, it pays not to appear too eager to please. That attitude leads to exploitation.

'I'll speak with Kat, my boss. I know she's heavy in debt. Once I explain it to her, she'll see this as an opportunity not to be missed. If it's all sweet, I'll text you tomorrow with the word "sweet".'

They look at each other for reassurance. You'd think they were a couple on a game show. As the host, I'm enjoying the entertainment.

'I need to know by tomorrow. You got a car for us yet?' Nines says, dropping from his perch.

'It's in hand,' I say.

'Have it ready in two days. I'll bung a grand on top.' With that, they crash out of the fire exit and into the night.

All's good in my world. I close the fire exit. Reaching behind my back, I remove the recording device strapped to me. I call Vince and update him on the state of play. He's over the moon. He's pleased I have the recording. All designed to create distance, for me, from Mike. I need Winter to think she'd misjudged me and Vince to continue his support of my role. Vince had his team hang back until Nines and Sugar have left the garage before following at a safe distance. I head home to the industrial site.

* * *

The gates open and shut behind me as I check the rearview mirror one last time before arriving at my unit. My unit door lifts, and I drive the Mini in. Mike's still on the coffee table. I must figure out where to scatter him.

After talking to Vince, he told me Little Chris has an Audi RS4 Avant for me to give to Nines. It does zero to sixty in four point one seconds thanks to a V6, three-litre, twin-turbocharged engine, and eight-speed auto gearbox. It's gunmetal-grey with low-profile alloy wheels and blacked-out rear windows. This will boost my credibility with the targets, confirming the benefits of keeping me on board.

Little Chris was gutted to hear it will be handed over to villains, but with the technical equipment being installed he hopes to get it back. The deadline for all the modifications will be met without me touching a welding torch.

I go to the safe and check all's well. The cash, passport, and gun are there. I take the gun and three clips. Better to be safe than sorry. I grab the whisky bottle.

The whisky chases down two tabs of morphine. I sit back and relax. The pistol is on the table. I feel safe.

My phones remain on the arm of my single seat. I take one last look at Mike's urn, shut my eyes, and wait for sleep.

16

Vince is with his outside team. Holly and I are sitting in her car, with one of Vince's police radios on, expecting to hear about the whereabouts of their targets – Spain aka Nines and Greece aka Sugar. When Vince told me he was deploying, I argued we needed to hear a live feed of how the targets reacted. Knowledge of the enemy is never wasted. I collected the radio after a team briefing at Hendon, enabling me to see all of Vince's surveillance vehicles. I wanted to stay alert to the chance of Vince switching targets and focusing on me. The radio comes to life:

> From Alpha Seven, subject Spain is out with subject Greece and they've got into vehicle, a VW Golf GTI. VRM to follow.

> Alpha Seven travelling north from Greece's home address, standby.

> Controller received. Radio silence unless active while Alpha Seven has contact, out.

The police radio comes to life with Alpha Seven commentating.

> Greece has gone into a Shell Station shop while Spain approaches cash machine, standby... Spain has deposited cash into the machine, amount unknown. Greece is still inside garage, standby... Greece is back in driver's seat. Spain back too. And vehicle away towards Crouch End.

The commentary continues and the same routine is described at another petrol station cash machine.

'What do you make of all that?' I say.

'I don't know,' Holly replies. 'It's strange they're depositing money rather than nicking it. Can you even do that? Vince will follow it up. We should learn something at the debrief.'

The surveillance team keeps with them until Nines and Sugar head back to Sugar's place. Vince stands them down and recalls them to Hendon. My phone goes; it's Vince.

'Get back to the garage. The Audi is on its way. It's plumbed up for sight and sound, so stay out of it unless operationally necessary. Show them the "tool" box and give Nines the key. It was a good run today. From what we've seen, we think they're using a crypto service to hide the money. Cash is deposited at the special machines, then it's converted to crypto currency. My bet is the end account won't be in their name. Speak later,' Vince says, ending the call.

Holly heard it all on speaker-phone. 'Clever bastards,' she says.

I smile at their ingenuity, then text Nines with the word "sweet". The toolbox Vince mentioned is a waterproof metal crate under the tyre mound where they'll store their guns and whatever they're using on the doors to the vans. Nines won't have the only key. Vince has another, and one will be left in the false air vent in the roof of the garage.

17

Rain clatters against the corrugated roof of the garage. The Audi is being offloaded along with a couple of other cars. I'm the tea boy while Holly signs off on the delivery. The driver of the lorry takes her clipboard, checks through each sheet for the signature, then tears off the top copy and hands it to her. All theatre designed to entertain any casual observer known to our targets.

The Audi is immaculate. No wonder Little Chris was weeping into his spanners when he got the release authority from Winter. I'm aware of Vince's instructions to stay out of the car, but he forgets that I'm going to be driving it, so I need to be aware of all the controls. The driver's door softly opens and closes. I sit in the driver's seat and look around. It's a perfect fit for us.

The alterations are good. Money is deposited in a box behind a fold-down arm that separates the back seat. There's an access hatch in the floor of the boot. They've had to sacrifice half the fuel tank to accommodate a hold for the weapons and cash. It's only for the eventuality that they get stopped by police. They'd never think of searching beyond what they can see. I could do with a car like this.

Holly comes over. 'Looks like the delivery didn't go unnoticed,' she says, leaving for the kitchen.

Nines and Sugar approach the garage door.

I step out of the car and begin wiping a rag over the bonnet as though I'd just finished polishing it.

'I hope this will do. It runs like a dream, top spec and serviced as you requested,' I say, as they get closer.

Nines gets in the passenger side and Sugar occupies the driver's seat.

'Nice. Very nice,' Sugar says.

'One thing?' Nines says.

'What?' I reply.

'What sound system has it got?' he says, nodding in appreciation of the wheels. 'You've done good, fuckin' good. The outside box works too. We laid the tools down last night. You're a magician.'

Praise indeed. It fills me with a sense of worth, a feeling I thought had died with Mike.

'As our lift has left, we'll take this,' Nines says.

I hand over the keys. No paperwork to sign for this delivery.

Nines and Sugar get in the car. The engine fires up and the Audi leaves the building. I send a text to Vince and let him know that the Audi is delivered. It's back to running a garage until contact is made from Nines or Vince.

* * *

We don't have to wait long. Thirty minutes later Holly's with me in the garage when her phone rings.

'Yes ... when?' She turns away as she speaks. 'How long? ... Okay, we'll await instructions.' She ends the call and turns back to me.

'Vince has asked if we could check the toolbox.'

I down the tools, grab the spare key from the safe space, and do as she requests. The guns are gone. Nines said he'd made use of the box last night. I recall seeing the Audi back out of the garage, then we closed the main doors so we could decompress after the handover. I close the lid, lock it, and return.

'The box is empty. They must have picked them up as they left. Can't he access the camera in the car remotely? See what's happening.'

'It's not responding to the mobile link. He's not going to be happy they're out with guns, too. He's nervous they've found out it's bugged.' Holly's eyes are locked on mine.

'You think I had something to do with it, don't you? You were with me when the car arrived, Holly. I briefly sat in the driver's seat, then got out. I never left you. They can't have found it. There's got to be an issue with the set-up. The tech guys can deal with it when they bring the car back to store it. They're not going to leave it on the street to get nicked. They want the equipment in one place. That's what they asked for.'

I turn away from her. She can't dispute the fact I was with her all the time. She gets back on the phone to Vince and updates him on our conversation. Then she stops talking and, placing the mobile back on her car bonnet, she turns to me.

'The tech guys say it was all working when it left them,' she says. 'That's not all. Vince had a call from the lines room. Nines has dropped his number. They've gone dark.'

I shrug. 'They're a professional outfit, Holly. It's unfortunate, but it isn't down to me. As for the in-car system, the tech guys fucked up the installation and are denying it to save face.' I start getting out of the overalls. This place has become tedious.

'Call if you hear anything. I've paperwork to do,' I say, chucking the overalls on the vehicle ramp before leaving by the fire exit. I could tell Holly was in no mood for a confrontation. She has no proof I did anything untoward. I get in the Mini and drive, confident I'm not being tailed. Vince will be trying to find the Audi. I turn into an access-only road and drive to the end.

Reaching under my seat, my fingers connect with gaffer tape. I pull it. It comes loose and I retrieve the small parcel it's attached to. Wrapped inside is an iPhone; it's contract free and a necessary tool of my trade. The phone powers up and accepts my face to access the apps I need. I find the one I'm after. A small red dot appears on the map screen. The dot is the Audi that Nines and his crew are out in.

I knew where the tech boys would install their monitoring link. The same place I taped my phone in my Mini. My brief time in the Audi was all I needed to put my own in and lose theirs.

When you know what you're feeling for, it can be retrieved quickly without drawing attention. I feel safer knowing I'm in control of it.

This operation was running too smoothly for me.

I exit the Mini and cross the road to dump the police tracker in a council bin. It's a small device and won't be recognised unless you know what you're looking at. It's also damaged beyond use. If Nines and his crew find mine, then that's easily explained away. The previous owners were conscious of it being stolen and took matters into their own hands to ensure it would be recovered. The one I used can be bought commercially.

The dot on my screen has stopped moving. I switch to satellite view and zoom in at street level, observing the name of the business premises coming up on the screen, street side. There's nothing obvious that would be worth robbing. I flick the screen to the left.

On the opposite side of them is a Tesco Metro. I highlight the address and search the web. It's open twenty-four-hours. A busy area. That means the returns are high. Cash collections will be constant.

I screenshot the image. I'm parked on a quiet side road. A young mum pushing a pram comes close. My presence could appear out of place. I engage the gearbox and head out towards my own lair.

18

Winter sits at the head of a conference table at New Scotland Yard. Vince and Holly are present. Satisfied they're settled, she begins the meeting.

'I appreciate you coming at short notice. I understand you're both operationally deployed, but this meeting couldn't wait.'

Vince and Holly nod.

'As you know,' Winter continues, 'the last operation ended in a way no one expected, with the suicide of Detective Superintendent Mike Hall. A very sad set of circumstances. Mike Hall was corrupt, and I still have concerns about DS Batford. Despite my best efforts to target these men, there hasn't been sufficient evidence to convict either. I wouldn't be doing my duty if I were to move on so quickly, as far as Batford is concerned.'

Winter opens a confidential docket and passes Vince and Holly a copy.

'The contents are for your eyes only,' Winter says.

Vince scans through the pages, then looks up at Winter.

'As you will learn,' Winter says, 'the docket contains sensitive information that a male known as Sky has been dealing in class A drugs and handling firearms. He has been working with another male known as Terry. Terry was the pseudonym Detective Superintendent Mike Hall used when he was a UC.'

Vince sits back, palm over the information sheet Winter was referring to. 'Come on, ma'am,' he says, 'this could be information from when Hall and Batford were legitimately working undercover. There's nothing here to say otherwise.' Vince shuts the file before he pushes it back to Winter.

Holly does the same.

'Vince, I know you don't want to think Batford is corrupt; you worked with him as a UC in the past. But the provenance of the information is tight as far as they're both concerned.' Winter sits back.

Vince raises his eyebrows and asks nothing further, understanding it would be unprofessional to ask where the information came from.

'What do you want us to do?' asks Holly. 'This is Professional Standards remit, ma'am. I was on the last operation, as you know, and I never witnessed Batford act corruptly. I would have raised it at the operational debrief.'

Winter leans forward, forearms on the desk, hands clasped in front. 'Commander Barnes asked me to brief you on this information in case you suspect corrupt practice during the current operation. We are dealing with a gang with access to explosives, firearms, and money. Vince, I acknowledge your stance, but I disagree with you. Holly, you're working closer to DS Batford than any of us. The need to prevent and detect crime must be a priority. That includes monitoring the actions of our own. I'll be your point of contact should any concern arise,' Winter says.

Vince remains unconvinced.

'What you're briefing us on is information from a source, known only to you. Information that's uncorroborated,' Vince says.

Holly adds nothing.

'Remain vigilant. Good luck with the rest of the operation. Let's get a result so we can move on to another job. They're backing up,' Winter says.

Vince and Holly get up and leave. Winter pours herself some water, then picks up her mobile and dials.

'Commander? Klara. They've been briefed as requested. Any further contact from Yvonne Hall? No ...

Okay, I'll make contact. We must be able to sink Batford with her on board. I'll let you know when I've handed her over to the Professional Standards source unit.' Winter ends the call, then rings Yvonne Hall to arrange a handover to her new source handler.

Sensitive log entry 30

Not the response I expected from either DI Gladwell or DC Burns at today's meeting. I'm aware Gladwell has worked with DS Batford in an undercover role, but his reluctance to see beyond the surface of Batford's practices is surprising. I'm aware Gladwell aspires to get promoted. His closed mind will have to open.

I acknowledge they don't know who the source of the information is. If they knew, I believe Gladwell would suggest she's making it up to alleviate any adverse attention on her family. But I have a good feeling Yvonne Hall will lead me to new evidence. Evidence to link Batford to corruption. She claims to have known Batford for several years.

A regular at dinner, that kind of thing. The only man connected to the job that Mike Hall ever brought home. "Treated him like the son he never had" were her words.

I make no excuses for being focussed on Batford. He's a disgrace to the exemplary service of the majority. The Metropolitan Police is one of the greatest police services in the world. Men like Batford don't belong. He needs locking up.

Organised crime won't die. It's getting stronger and more effective whilst the capacity to police the streets diminishes. I will not tolerate corruption. Yvonne provides the opportunity I need to destroy Batford and Hall's empire for good.

Entry complete.

Klara Winter – Detective Superintendent
Authorising officer
Covert policing
Op Envy

19

The evening shift has appeared on the landing. Washing is being collected from laundry dollies that line the walls. I find the key for my new door and enter the flat. The flat's been tidied. On the table is a note from Olivia:

> Thank you, I'm okay now, and back next door. X.

I enter the kitchen and check the cupboards for drinks. The whisky's still there. I take a mug, a strip of morphine, and indulge myself. My phone vibrates on the arm of the chair. It's Holly.

'Where are you?' she says, abruptly.

'Who wants to know?'

'I do, you prick!'

'I'm at the flat.'

There's a pause before she replies. 'Good. I'm coming up.'

The line goes dead.

There's a knock at the door and she enters, overalls bundled under her arm. She's casually dressed in skinny jeans and a white T-shirt. I offer her a drink, which she accepts, flopping down into the two-seater sofa. I hand her the drink and leave the bottle on a side table.

'What's with the home visit? Don't trust me to be where I say I am?'

She shakes her head.

'Why are you here?' I say.

She sets her glass down, leans back, and curls her feet under her backside.

'I'm bored sitting around while you do all the negotiations. I feel like a blown bulb in a lighthouse.' She picks up her drink, observing me over the rim of the glass as she takes a sip.

'You must have been on jobs where the bad guys bond to one of us more than the other?' I say.

There's a knock at the door.

Nines and Sugar leer back at me through the spyhole.

I let them in, checking the landing each way as I do. They go to the living room where Holly says hello in her Kat persona. I go to the kitchen.

'Hey, bring in another two glasses, will ya?' Sugar says to me.

I find a couple of mugs. They'll have to make do with that. When I enter the lounge, there's a hand-drawn map laid out on the table. They're clearly relaxed in our company. I pass the mugs and pour for each of them.

'Planning a road trip?' I say to break the ice. A low ripple of laughter fills the room.

'Funny man,' Nines says. 'We've got a bit of work on, but we're a pair of hands light. Thought we'd offer you first dibs.' Nines taps the map. 'It's all here: times, locations, drop-off points. Piece of piss.'

'What's the job and how many people have you been to with this proposal?' Holly says, directing the question at Nines.

I'm glad she's involving herself like this. I've told Nines she'll be cool with me working with them. Holly will feedback to Winter and Vince that I'm a team player. Which team, is for me to decide.

'You're it, darling. We're choosy who we share our spoils with.'

'What do you need from us?' Holly says.

'I'm down a man,' Nines replies.

'And what makes you think either of us would be a suitable replacement?' Holly asks.

Nines shifts in the dining room chair he's got himself comfortable in. I shoot her a glance. Too many questions are never a good idea.

'I see it like this,' Nines says. 'If either of you refuse to come out to play, your business will suffer. Ain't that right, Sugar?'

Sugar smiles.

'Are you threatening me?' Holly asks Nines. She leans forward, taking no shit.

'I don't work on threats, love. I work on certainty. What I can tell you, for certain, is your business will suffer and suffer badly. But hey, it's your call at the end of the day but it's important to me you know how we operate so there's no confusion. Fixing cars is one thing, but I need hands on deck.' Nines leans back and salutes Holly and me with his mug of whisky.

'What do you want?' I say.

Sugar chips in. 'We need a driver. I figure you'll do, Mr Sky, if your boss is amenable to letting you do some night work and the occasional afternoon?'

I look at Holly.

'Like Nines said, I don't have any choice', she says. 'If you get nicked, Sky, then you don't mention my place to the filth. It's all I have.' She carries on drinking.

Nines pushes the map to me. 'Study it, then get rid of it,' he says. 'You'll get twenty minutes' notice when I need you. That includes getting the Audi and scooping us two up. Keep the Audi close for the next week or so. It's a nice ride. You done well.'

Nines and Sugar get up, downing what's left of their drinks and leaving the mugs.

They're walking out when Nines turns back to face us. 'Last thing before we go. Don't go getting ideas about talking to Five-Oh. I've got eyes and ears everywhere.

Keep your heads down and all will be cool. Olivia was seen to come in here, Sky. Her owners didn't like that. I straightened it out with them, so all is good for you on that count.'

Sugar throws me the Audi keys. 'It's at the garage. It'll need fuel.'

They leave, shutting the main door to the flat.

Holly turns her attention to me. 'Who's Olivia?'

I stand up and gather the mugs.

'Olivia's a kid who lives next door. She was getting a good kicking and needed sanctuary. I left her here and stayed at the garage. That's all.'

'You've had a kid in police protection inside a covert flat? Nice one.'

'Not exactly. She said she's eighteen, but I have my doubts.' I'm beyond caring what Holly thinks. As far as I'm concerned, Olivia is an adult. That's what she told me.

Holly accepts that conversation is over and carries on drinking.

'So, what makes you their driver, then? What have you got that I haven't?' She's smiling, but the question is a loaded one.

'In a word, bollocks. You could, undoubtedly, be the better driver. You know that. Nines doesn't though. I reckon Nines sees you as the brains. You own the business. I'm the lackey.'

I sit back and rub my scalp. The closeness of another human being in the same flat as me is a rare occurrence. I feel like I've forgotten how to act out of role.

I know how to act among those I infiltrate, but not those on my police side – the good side, for what it's worth to me.

Holly smirks. 'Still,' she says between giggles, 'we'd better not talk to the cops though, we have been warned…'

She sends whisky down her chin as her head leans back in uncontrollable laughter. Her laughter becomes infectious. For the first time in a long while, I surrender to the joy of the moment.

* * *

My head feels heavy. I can smell coffee. I'm on the sofa. A blanket is over me. I try to get myself together and remember who was here last night. Holly appears from the kitchen wearing a T-shirt. It falls above the knees of her naked legs.

She puts the coffee down on the floor beside me and gracefully sits in the chair opposite.

'Morning, stud. You ride like a biker — all hands and plenty of throttle.' She brings her legs up on the chair, tucking them under her.

I know she's playing with me. I'm fully dressed and remember the state she was in before I passed out.

'One of your favourite bands?' Holly says, pulling the bottom of the T-shirt she's wearing to show a pop band I don't know.

'It isn't mine.'

'Whose is it then? It's in your flat?'

'I don't know. It was insecure, remember? Anyone could have dossed down here,' I say.

It can only be Olivia's. Despite Nines' reassurance, I'm not convinced he had her welfare at heart. I can't be the last person to see her. Olivia is a problem I don't need. This is what happens when you do the right thing, or wrong thing in my case, as it may turn out.

'Try explaining that to Vince,' Holly says.

'Like I said, not my problem. There's a clean T-shirt of mine, in the bathroom. Take that.' I tell her.

I get up and enter my bedroom thankful it's still in the same made state I'd left it in. I lie back on the bed, giving her some privacy.

'Leave the one you've got on here. Mine's plain, so you won't have any explaining to do with your mates,' I shout out to her.

I can hear the water running. She doesn't reply.

She's singing. She has a good voice for a shower singer. Times like these remind me of the scarcity of normality in my life. I have little downtime. When I do, I squander it through medication, drink, or both.

I'm not a drunk or an addict. I have control of what I put inside me. It's the quickest way I know to switch off and feel the tension drain from my limbs and muscles.

The singing stops. I hear the bathroom door go. Holly appears, framing the bedroom, wrapped in a towel. I'm transfixed.

'Were you saying something? I couldn't hear you properly,' she says.

'There's a T-shirt in the bathroom. Use it. I have another,' I say.

'Seen it, thanks. Not my usual shade of black, but what's a girl to do when she's stayed away all night in a man's flat?' With that, she pushes lightly away from the doorframe.

We leave, taking her car.

20

It's midday. Nines left the Audi at the side of the garage. There are no customers waiting. Word is out we're not to be messed with while the gang is working with us. We've been accepted among the people we're targeting.

I'm conscious of an innate desire to move on with my life. To get out of the police. The pain of this feeling eats away at my gut like a fetid sore. Winter's net is drawing in. She won't stop until I'm hauled in by her corporate trawler.

I have more than enough money to survive. I have Mike's industrial facility and a residential flat I'm yet to see.

I could sell the lot and leave everything behind. Cash in my chips. I've lost all sense of self doing this job. It's a vocation that consumes you – changes you.

I should never have been the bent cop I am. The harder I try to change, the more I can't. The criminal side of my brain has overtaken my every waking moment to the point where I couldn't even protect Olivia, a young person in need. I left a vulnerable human being in a shitty estate flat with an insecure door and a mob seeking to exploit her. This is something I'll need to address.

Holly interrupts my brooding.

'There's no point both of us being stuck here nursing a hangover,' she says. 'I've got other work on, so I'm returning to the office. Why don't we both call in when one of us gets something? I may suggest to Winter that I introduce another undercover in and then exit. I'm spare on this, and we both know it.'

I thought Holly had shaken this off last night, I was wrong.

'If you leave, they could spook. I'll be objecting to your decision to Winter if you play that card. I need to prove that I'm not like Mike. The only way I can do that is for you to watch me work.' I leave that hanging. Hopefully she'll see sense.

Sometimes it's necessary for the hunted, me, to draw the hunter in to get a clean kill. That's my intention. I have my methods of eliminating those who can't work with me.

'That surprises me. I thought you'd encourage me to go?' Holly says.

'It shows how little we know each other. Update Winter and Vince. I'll call you as soon as I get any contact from Nines,' I say.

She agrees, then leaves. I need to check out the flat Mike left me. Things have a habit of escalating rapidly in these situations. I can't have all my eggs in one basket at the industrial site. Once Holly is gone, I get a minicab to drop me within a short walking distance of the industrial site.

The more I think about it, the more I can see that Mike must have known our empire was collapsing. He didn't set out to top himself that day with Razor. He thought he was leaving for a warmer climate where he and Razor would carry on and I would be left to make my own choices. The recorded message was his way of saying he was dead to everyone. Little did he know he would be. He wanted to ensure I'd be looked after despite his willingness to see me dead. Like a doting father with a psychopathic disorder.

I decide on the Porsche for today's jaunt. I change into plain jeans and a grey T-shirt. My footwear isn't befitting the vehicle, but Converse it is. I can play that off against the need to fit it over the prosthetic. It'll add to the tale of injury compensation helping me to afford the car, should those kinds of questions be raised or mooted.

I start up the Porsche. The unit's main shutter door opens, and I exit towards the city.

I continually check my mirrors as I leave the main gate, stopping, pulling over, changing lanes, and using roundabouts like a lost tourist. The Nines' line rings. I answer on speakerphone.

'Where you at? You're never at fucking work, man.' Nines' voice infiltrates the car.

'You're not my boss, but you're beginning to sound a lot like her. What's up?'

'That's where you're wrong, bruv. While we have our arrangement, if I say bark, you start yipping.' Nines has company. I can hear laughter and the unmistakable sounds of pool or snooker balls hitting each other. I ignore his comments.

'Where are you?' I say.

'Wood Green, playing pool. I sent a runner to the garage. They told me it was shut. Come down. The Taverna is the place. I got some work.'

'I'm on the North Circular near Tottenham. See you soon.' I head in the direction of Bounds Green. I ditch the Porsche and get a cab to Turnpike Lane. The Taverna is a restaurant in Green Lanes.

The smells coming from the place are more enticing than the prospect of the pool hall above it. I don't call Vince or Holly. This could be good for me. I can't afford delays waiting for a cover team from Vince. I need to weigh Nines up in an environment he's comfortable in. I'm good with a cue, but not when it comes to potting balls.

Families eat, chatting, sharing meze dishes in a relaxed atmosphere. I enter and walk towards a rear door.

There's a set of wooden steps. As I approach, a rodent of a man gets up from a side table and places his tattooed fingers on my chest. I choose to wait and see what he has in mind. He makes the universal motion for me to raise my arms. I oblige. He pats me down, turning my body around as he frisks me. He's attentive. Not settling for my top half only.

He stops as his hands clasp the titanium of my lower left leg. He reacts as though he's had an electric shock. I gently pull up my jean leg, revealing the prosthetic. Satisfied, he waves me through. I see him pick up a Motorola handheld radio and press "transmit". I ascend the stairs to a room above the restaurant. There's a door up top that's shut. I knock. A girl opens it. I say girl – she's in her early twenties, olive skin, with a set of teeth so bright they could warn ships in a storm. She invites me in. I see Nines and Sugar with two unknowns at a pool table.

A small bar area supports two champagne buckets. A couple of spent bottles plus two new ones wrapped at the neck in white linen. The girl takes one of the bottles and pours four fresh glasses, wiping away the residue on the neck. These boys are either celebrating a successful outing or toasting to the future. Time will tell.

I accept the glass flute and join the others at their table of choice. A new triangle is out, and balls racked ready to break.

The heat from the overhead table lights is strong.

We're not alone. Three other tables are occupied by a group of Turks. Their looks in my direction make it known they've clocked me. New faces are obviously a rare sight. This could get lively. Nines motions me over.

'You came alone?'

'Yeah. Kat's busy.' I take in my surroundings, planning where I can exit quickly. Nines lights up a spliff. He offers me an unlit one. I take it. We move back to the bar, leaving Sugar and the two unknowns to carry on the game.

'Light up and chill. We're here for a good time, not a long time,' Nines says, as he looks at my spliff and offers up a light. I move the spliff away from the flame.

'I'll save it for later. I never partake where business is being discussed. I prefer a clear head,' I say.

Nines' head moves back like he's attached to a lead that's just been yanked. His eyes are on mine. The spliff could be a test to see if I'm police. I don't get that impression, though. He wouldn't have brought me here to test that theory. Too many witnesses and the clientele wouldn't appreciate him introducing a cop to an invite-only club.

'Suit yourself. I'll take the smoke out of your wages,' he says.

We sit at the bar and the hostess makes herself scarce. Nines is relaxed. He's not pissed, but he's been enjoying the party.

'What am I here for?' I say.

Nines shifts on his stool, takes a long draw, and blows out the smoke.

'We're celebrating a job well done. Toots is history, ya get my drift?'

I get his drift all right. Nines, or someone on his say-so, has had him relocated to the land of no return.

'The shooting the other day outside your gaff was down to him,' Nines continues. 'He weren't on the trigger, but the kid who let the round off was keen to talk once it was made crystal clear he didn't have long left to live if he didn't. Toots put him up to it for fifty quid! Fifty fuckin' quid for my life? An insult.'

He pauses and drinks. I do the same. The others in the room aren't paying any attention to us.

'You killed him?' I say with an expectation of being dismissed or blanked. I do have a role to perform after all.

'Let's say Toots and his fam have moved on. The kid on the bike took the message like a man; hand-delivered it to Toots. That's history now. There's a job I want you on tomorrow,' he says, then leans in.

I so want to take a draw. The sweet scent of dried herbal leaf, is as seductive as the scent of a lover. "Lover" – the word reminds me of Stoner, a woman who knew how to party and handle a criminal. My body aches for medication. I feel alone. Sometimes medicating the pain of isolation is all I want. My old back-up – though as weak as the fading sun – is now gone. Mike was more to me than I realised.

I snap out of it and get back to business. 'What's the job and where do I come in?' I ask. I need this work. I must test myself. Flip the coin and see if I still land corrupt side up.

'We're gonna make some cash deposits. I need you behind the wheel should we get any unwanted attention,' Nines says.

'You're depositing money, not taking it?'

'That's right. We don't use conventional banking methods. Them days are gone, bruv. We've moved into the digital era. Turning green to gold.' He laughs.

The background music increases in volume as the hostess returns behind the bar.

Nines is a crypto man. The deposit he's referring to means cash machine points at designated sites. Money goes in and is converted to crypto, the anonymous person's choice of banking. I admire his style.

To look at him, he seems nothing more than an older-generation street punk, but there's a business brain there and he's doing well. He must have got dyed money at some point and that would need washing.

I glance at the Turks. They're keeping themselves to themselves, but my gut tells me they must be part of the operation, or they wouldn't be here while Nines openly discusses this part of the business. Vince and Winter will need this, all of it.

I know Vince will want to talk about a plan of action now Holly will have talked to him; maybe she's still with him.

My mind turns back to Nines. 'What time and where?' I ask.

'Tomorrow. I'll get a runner to come to your flat in the early hours. Bring the Audi,' he says.

I can't use the Audi. That would be an unwarranted risk. Vince may have been working on getting it back online and not telling me. He hasn't confronted me about it though.

I know Vince. He's not like me. First sniff I was corrupt he'd nick me himself and claim I struggled on arrest. It wouldn't be pretty.

'Not the Audi. It's too valuable for this type of job. We'll use mine, less attention.'

'I like your way of thinking,' Nines says. 'My mind's a bit fucked now, but it'll clear later. It won't take long, but there's lots of cash to clear.' He raises his glass and I reciprocate.

* * *

Holly is waiting for Vince to bring the coffees over. She is glad she arrived twenty minutes before the agreed time to grab a table.

Vince puts down the coffees and sits next to her. 'The BMW's secure. Forensics are at work on it,' he says.

'Good. Sam's flat door is back on.'

'He told you that?'

'I was there last night.'

Vince raises his eyebrows.

'It's good for the people on the estate to see me,' she says. 'Plus, I needed to kick back with him. See what he's like when he's not on duty.'

Vince leans closer to her. 'The faulty tracker in the Audi bothers me. They were out with weapons on that occasion. The camera from the box they were stored in captured Nines lifting the gun. It also shows them putting the weapons back.'

'You don't think Sam's tampered with the tracker, do you? When would he have done that? I was with him,' Holly says.

Vince shrugs. 'I'm keeping an open mind.'

'I know what Winter thinks of him. That meeting she called us to, said it all. From what I'm seeing, he's doing everything as it should be done. Look at the recording of his meeting with Nines at the garage. He wanted backup in case the garage equipment didn't pick up the conversation.'

'Sam's a shrewd cookie, Holly. Don't underestimate him. I've got to leave. You're doing a great job. Keep your wits about you. I have as good a control as I can on this lot. My teams are armed and I'll call the strike if life is threatened. In the meantime, we work as we are. High-risk tactics require high-risk players. My team is just that. I include you and Sam in that equation, too.' Vince downs his coffee and they both leave.

21

I left Nines to do his thing. There's no word from Holly. I'm back in the Porsche and check the sat nav. I'm near to where my new home is situated. I won't have long there, just enough to see what Mike's left me and whether it's worth the risk. Mike was adamant it's only known to him, but that doesn't provide me with a feeling of safety or reassurance.

I weave the Porsche through the width restriction at The Spaniards Inn and follow the edge of Hampstead Heath to the ponds. I do a circle of the roundabout, then head past the tube.

People are making the most of an unseasonably warm evening, sat outside fancy cafés sipping wine.

The finish line to my destination approaches. I take a side street. The sat nav announces that the address is to my right. I don't slow, keeping my speed appropriate for a residential street. Expensive cars line each side of the road. The Porsche isn't flash enough to be distinctive here. The sat nav announces my arrival outside a black iron gate that spans a circular driveway. The Edwardian house is split in two. I hope Mike chose the ground floor accommodation. I have a key with a fob attached.

Leaving the Porsche down the road, I walk towards the premises on the opposite footway, paying attention to a couple behind me. There's a tension between them I don't like. Maintaining my pace, I make use of vehicle mirrors and windows to catch fleeting observations of the pair. A black saloon, like many used by those in the CID, enters the street.

The couple slows down. My heart rate increases. I remind myself I've done nothing wrong. I hear the female's footsteps speed up. The saloon slows as it approaches me. I move behind a parked Transit van as though I'm looking to cross the road.

I hear the saloon stop abruptly. Shouts of "Police – stop!" shatter the peaceful ambience. I must have been tailed by Winter. She must have known about the flat and was waiting for me to make my move. There's no way out of this. Even if I ditch the keys, she'll lock the street down and have a POLSA team on hands and knees looking for them.

I take a deep breath, step out from behind the van, and wait for the shouts to increase and for the officers to assume their position as I get nicked. As I enter the road, I see that other people have appeared. The couple are bent over the saloon's bonnet, arms up their backs, wrists straining as handcuffs are snapped on. A young detective is requesting a van unit via his radio. My breathing goes back to normal, and I continue towards the gated driveway. Trust Mike to pick a crime hot spot to buy a flat.

I press the fob against a pedestrian access gate. It clicks open and I step through. The gate shuts behind me with a reassuring clunk. I'm safe in my suburban cage. I approach a large front door. On its right is another pad like that on the gate. I hold the fob against it and the door unlocks. It opens onto a black-and-white chequered tiled floor.

The house has all the charm of a private medical practice and not the home it presents itself as from the outside. An internal door opens into a small hallway. At the end of the short hall is a reinforced door. On the sidewall is a small keypad unit – a secure key box I have no number for.

I start thinking like Mike, and where he would have left the code. There's no way he'd have remembered it. He struggled to recall his own secure login details for his covert computer. I feel around the box. Underneath, my fingers touch sticky tape. A small piece of paper comes away. It's in Mike's handwriting. The code is nine, nine,

nine. He had a sense of humour after all. I punch in three nines and open the box, retrieve the final door key, and step inside.

The carpeted hallway is a welcome sight after the vinyl tiles of my estate digs. The place feels like an opulent panic room. Small screens are situated at different locations on the wall. As I pass one, it illuminates showing light, air conditioning, and remote curtains settings.

A doorway off the hall reveals an open-plan living area, minimal in furnishing but what's here isn't from Ikea. This is where Mike invested good money. He must have used the riverside flat as a front, confirming what Yvonne told me. He was willing to give all that up.

He was never flash at work. The Thameside apartment wasn't him. He was playing with the police. Once they seized that, they'd think they'd struck gold.

I can see him at home here. Slouched in the huge sofa, tie off, whisky in hand, and watching some shit on TV while he shouted at the screen. There's an envelope on a drinks table. It contains a small controller and a set of instructions. I do as it says and, on pressing the power button on the controller, a false wall moves revealing his favourite cinema-size TV. Another button makes the screen come to life and before me is his grinning drug and alcohol fuelled mug. Yet another message from beyond the grave.

His tie is where it usually sat, halfway down his chest. His right hand is wrapped round a whisky tumbler and a Cuban cigar nestles in his mouth.

'If you're watching this, you've worked out the code to the door, which, by the way, I purposefully made easy for you. I know what you're like with numbers.' He pauses while he laughs at his own joke. 'I hope you like the place, Sam. You deserve a good home. I recorded this message and left one at the industrial unit. Every time I left either place, I set this recording up to be played. I never knew if I'd make it back to either. Hopefully, what I've left will be enough to see my debt to you repaid. I don't know what you'll do. Go straight or branch out. The job's fucked, Sam. You may as well take what you can. No one gives a flying fuck about you. I did. I want you to know that. I was weak where you were strong.

'Thing is, Sam, when you get the taste for the good life, you can't go back. To go back would be a waste of your skill set. We took from the scum who defile our city and had a good life along the way. We're grafters, drifters, rebels – men of worth. We know the villains we dealt with never saw any real jail time. Why waste our time with all the paperwork? Hit them where it hurts. Walk away with what they coveted.

'If you can't handle this anymore and want shot of both places, then tell my brief. She'll deal with it. She's getting a good wedge for her service. Whatever you decide, she'll sort it. Have a drink on me and make your choice. It's your favourite bottle. Best house-warming gift I could get at short notice. Well, there's not much more I can say. Sam, you're a marked man in and out of the police. Don't get greedy like me, Sam, but don't sell yourself short. My solicitor's details and direct number are in the cutlery drawer.' He sits back and drinks a full tumbler, wiping his mouth at the end as he pulls on the knot of his tie.

'One last thing,' he adds, with his eyes set in a hard stare at the screen, the same look he'd get before he issued one of his ultimatums. 'I think Yvonne's talking to the police. Some of the other jobs didn't go so well. I may have said too much in her company. I never got nicked, but shipments got seized that should have run to plan. Be careful around her. Londoners need people like you and me to clean up the mess. Now go and do your work.'

He leans forward. His face freezes as the recording stops. His eyes are wet. I fill my glass, sit back, and have one last drink with the man I once called a friend, while I contemplate my future.

22

I'd left the bunker, as I've chosen to name my newly acquired home, to spend the evening in my estate flat. Seeing Mike spooked me. I needed to get out. I feel like Mike's hostage. Even in death, he's controlling me like a dealer tracks their shipment. Press-ups, sit-ups, and dips do nothing to calm me.

My phones are laid out on the table. I keep checking them. I'm sweating, yet I feel cold. I need Nines to call tonight. I must get out. Feel the night air.

The screen on the phone flashes with Nines' name. I take the call, recognising his voice immediately.

'We're good to go. Be ready in ten. I'll send a runner.' The line goes dead.

His runner arrives. He leads the way down to the parking area by my block. He knows my car. He stops by it as we wait for Nines. He tells me to open my car and get in. While he waits outside, he puts a call in. Nines appears from another vehicle parked six cars down and ducks into mine, slinging a bag in the backseat. It looks heavy.

The runner taps the roof and becomes a ghost.

'Just us then?' I say. It works in my favour having him here alone.

'Sugar is in another motor. Don't get any ideas. He's strapping and knows how to use it if he needs to,' Nines says.

'Where to?' I say.

'Follow what it says on here.' Nines shows me another smartphone. The female voice on the GPS announces where I should turn. I look at Nines, then drive where directed.

Sugar is driving behind me. There's little traffic due to the early hour of the morning. I can only think Nines has chosen 0300 hours to conduct business as there'll be fewer cops on the street. The only issue I have is that any cop with an ounce of tenacity to nick villains will notice us and know we need turning over. Tonight isn't the night I want flipping like a pancake.

* * *

Regent's Park is deserted; no runners, only the odd urban fox makes an appearance.

I'm reminded of when I was about to kill a guy called Hamer, the bent accountant of a ruthless Italian gangster whom I was purporting to work for. The feral eyes of the animal had caught mine as I was about to set Hamer alight. I escaped, as did the fox. Hamer's a different story. I've come a long way since then and my desire to fulfil my calling is still an ever-present danger.

'Yo, you missed the first stop,' Nines yells, shattering my memory of past nocturnal adventures.

I U-turn and wait opposite a petrol station. Nines takes a bundle of notes and puts them in a carrier bag. He looks about, then takes out a cheap burner phone.

Sugar has stopped further back. The rear door of his car opens. A different runner approaches Nines' side. Nines lowers his window and passes the bag through, along with an iPhone. Nines is using different phone lines. The iPhone is only for the crypto currency. The runner will have his own phone. If they get nicked, the iPhone will be clean of any call data and they'll be on their own when explaining why they have it. I keep the engine running and concentrate on the environment. There's only one person at the service hatch of the petrol station. He's unsteady on his feet, propping himself up against the wall. The attendant is looking hassled as he brings packets of cigarettes to the night hatch.

The runner strolls confidently over to a cash machine, conducts a final look about, places the smartphone screen near the cash machine's monitor and starts feeding in the cash. The garage forecourt staff pays no attention. The last note slides in. A small sheet of paper ejects, and he puts it in his pocket. He checks the iPhone then returns to our car and hands it back to Nines along with a receipt that has a QR code on it.

I'd been so busy concentrating on the cash feeder that I'd missed the pistol resting between Nines' knees.

Nines clocks me noticing and smiles.

'Risky business these cash drops, you know what I'm saying?' he says, with his youthful grin while the runner returns to Sugar's car. 'Let's go to the next one.'

The smoothness of the operation astonishes me. Despite the firepower he's carrying, he coolly waits while his runner is let loose with thousands of pounds' worth of notes to feed into a machine in a service station in London. There are cameras everywhere, yet he's indifferent to the risk. The police could drive in and fill up, too. He's not fazed.

'What if we've been seen on the cameras? They're everywhere at these stations,' I say.

Nines looks out of his window. 'The cameras are off. The Turks from the pool club control the staff at the forecourts. The machine is managed by your neighbours. People I choose to invest my money with. It wasn't cool what you did with that girl at your flat. Those Russians are nervous about the Turks looking to take over their empire. The Russians don't trust you. They think you're employed by the Turks to feedback on what's going on. I invited you to the Taverna because the Russians wanted you checked out. The Turks asked a shitload of questions when you left. The Russians have a grass in the club who saw how things were. They reported back that it didn't look staged. You passed the test. That's why you're with me and not in a grave thanks to the Russians,' he says.

'I appreciate the heads-up,' I say.

I respect his work but, now he's confirmed he's close to the Russians, I have every intention of destroying what they're building.

When I'm finished, they'll be history.

As I pull out of the service station, a marked police response car pulls in behind us and heads towards the pumps. I check my mirror and observe the driver glance at us then at his dashboard. His operator is talking into a radio and looking at the back of my Mini. I assume he's running my plate. Overhead, a street light flickers, and dies. I turn to Nines.

'Don't look behind. We've got company. Sit tight, belt up, and ditch the piece.'

Nines has already seen what I've seen. He's texting Sugar. I glance over as he types "Five-Oh" and hits send. Another marked unit has come into play. There'll be more soon. Backup has been called. It has the hallmarks of a three-car hard-stop.

I need to move and fast, or we'll be kettled in on the station forecourt. I roll towards the exit like any other driver merging onto a main road. The marked car behind us mimics the move. He's not filling up.

Sugar begins a U-turn. The second police car takes the bait and spins round in his direction.

I see a black cab coming and wait my turn. There's a flash of headlights behind and a flick of the blue strobe. The cab gets closer. I wait for the moment to make my break. It must be slick. There'll be no room for error.

Fifty feet, there's another flash of the blue strobe followed by a blip of the two tones. I engage the drive and floor our car ahead of the cab. The cop car has read the tactic. He attempts to jump with me, but I feed him the cab in one slick move, blocking the exit as we make off. The engine feels strong and the Mini handles well. We're lighter than the cop car, too.

The cop car is fully lit. Strobe lights pulsate and bounce off my internal mirror. I dip it to anti-glare. Nines is looking for somewhere to ditch the gun.

'The speaker grill comes off. Remove it and chuck the gun in the door panel,' I shout.

Nines hesitates.

'Fuck that. I'm gonna do them.' He starts to lower the window. I take a sharp left through a red light. The momentum throws Nines off balance, and he knocks into my shoulder as the car rocks but maintains a straight line towards Finsbury Park.

'Lose the fucking gun,' I shout.

The sound of sirens echoes around us.

'We need to get away,' I yell, 'not start a fucking war with the filth.'

He looks at me and tries the speaker grill, which comes away with two pulls. The Mini grips the road and weaves through the minimal traffic as I make progress away from the lead police car. I must avoid the main routes if I'm to survive. It's the early hours and cops will be up for a chase. I slow and draw the cop car in closer.

'What the fuck are you slowing down for? Get us the fuck out of here!' Nines yells.

From the side mirror, all I can see are bright halogen lights and blue neon beams bearing down on us. I wait. The cops are getting closer and closer.

The headlights invade the interior of our car. Nines pulls his hood up. I already have a hood up.

Green Lanes approaches. The kebab shop opposite has a gaggle of drunks late-night feeding; their attention shifts from ordering to our sideshow. The cop car is close enough to ram me. He'll be looking to end the pursuit – I would be.

At the junction, I drop the left indicator for Green Lanes. The cop car drops back in preparation to turn. I press the Mini's fog light button twice. I see the red illuminate the windscreen of the cop car. The driver takes the bait and slows, mistaking my fog lights for brake lights.

I turn to the left and maintain my speed. I take my finger off the fog lights and press it back on quickly. The driver reacts, thinking I'm about to stop, bail out, and run.

I floor the car right. The cop car swerves left. I carry on straight. I kill our lights and take a left into Eade Road and stop in a vacant driveway.

'Get down. Don't look up until I tell you,' I say.

Nines does as I say. Sirens can be heard. A wave of blue lights and reflective blue and yellow livery race along the street we're in. Headlights sweep the road. We're not safe, yet.

A cop car moves slowly along the street – headlights sweeping the tarmac like a prison searchlight. I stay as low as I can across Nines' legs, and he does the same behind my back.

An engine sound grows louder as a car gets closer. The lights get brighter. The smell of our thrashed engine permeates the car through the internal air filter. There's no way out or back.

I prepare myself for the inevitable. I'd done my best to evade our pursuer, but I'm deep in the shit – stuck in a car with a known armed robber and a handgun, having evaded police. Winter will be rubbing her hands at the prospect of my arrest. I can justify what's happened to her if I get nicked. Whether she accepts my word or not, is out of my control.

Nines says nothing. All I can hear is our breathing as we recover from the adrenaline rush of the chase. My legs shake; I wait and hope.

The lights stop casting a glare into our car. The engine idles. I hear car doors opening and closing – three, to be exact; the driver waiting inside, no doubt. I should have bluffed the cop at the petrol station but the benefit of hindsight is not helping the situation now. A torchlight shines into the front of our car. I sit up, showing my hands as the door is opened.

'What in the fuck are you doing on my drive?' A rough male voice says from behind the phone torch that's shone in my face. I keep my hands where he can see them.

From his shadow, he's clearly a big lump and from the sound of the doors, he must have company.

'We were just leaving,' I say.

As he lowers the torch. My eyes adjust. I smile at him.

'Give me your car keys or I'll introduce you to my favourite hammer.' To emphasise his point, he shows the claw hammer he's brandishing in his shovel-sized fist.

'You're the boss, mate. Here're the keys. Let's not get stupid.' I move to get the keys and then I hear Nines.

'Shift your motor from behind us and let us leave.' Nines has the pistol aimed at the guy who hadn't noticed him move due to his concentration on me. Nines hadn't used the speaker hole after all.

The guy backs up, drops the hammer, and moves towards his car. He gets in and reverses, making room for me to move out. I reverse and stop alongside him, driver to driver. I indicate for him to wind his window down and he does, albeit with caution.

'Your house is safe. We've done nothing wrong,' I say.

The guy nods, with a look of shock on his face.

'Where are your mates?' I say.

'It's just me, just me. I opened and shut the doors to make anyone in your car think there was more than me,' he says.

I'm impressed.

'Good skills. I trust this will go no further. We know where you live,' I say.

I drive and leave the street. The search for us is over; other matters will be requiring police attention. But the Mini's too risky to be out in now.

'I'm dumping this car,' I say. 'Let's find a cab and get home.'

Nines agrees. I park it up and we get out.

'We'll split here. That guy has placed us together. If he calls the police, we're fucked.'

Nines agrees again and stuffs the gun down the back of his waistband.

'That's cool with me,' he says. 'I'll let you know tomorrow when the next bit of work is on. You done good tonight, well good. You'll be in the Audi for the next job. Then you'll know what we're all about. I just got a text from Sugar. They lost the filth too.'

He leaves in the opposite direction from me. I know it's early in the morning, but I send a text to Little Chris at the garages for him to arrange for the Mini to get collected and sort me another car. I'll miss that motor. Reliability is a rare commodity in my world. I walk the street in hope of a taxi to flag down and a ride away from a job well done.

23

'Where were you last night? I tried getting hold of you, but there was no reply,' Holly says. She looks up from a computer she's working on.

'I fell asleep,' I say.

She doesn't ask anything else. We're in an office at Hendon waiting on the arrival of Vince and Winter for a debrief and update.

I have important news. I know a Turkish firm is in collaboration with a group of Russian people traffickers who happen to be my neighbours.

I hear the unmistakable laugh of Vince in the corridor.

The office door beeps as the entry code unlocks it. Both he and Winter enter like gladiators into the arena. I look up and acknowledge their presence, then carry on with my computer searches.

Vince does the honours with the kettle, then we all settle down in a cosy corner, or "the meeting bay" as it's officially known. Vince gestures to Winter, and she gets the meeting going.

'We appear to be making progress thanks to Vince's work. His source unit has heard that Toots has disappeared. Rumours of a hit, but no one is confirming. He is reported as missing but his absence means there's an opening on Nines' crew. We're interested in finding out who is taking over Toots' role, when they recruit, and where they intend to hit next. As of today, we have a line on Nines. Despite this now being in place, Commander Barnes and I still view you both as proportionate and necessary resources.' Winter takes a breath and a drink.

Vince takes over.

'We'll be working off this line for a while. Troops on the ground will be stretched as another job's come in requiring my surveillance resources.'

This gets my attention.

Vince continues, 'When my teams deploy, they will be armed. From all we've learnt to date, I think Nines is looking for a big hit. So, keep doing what you're doing. Show your faces at the garage daily. Sam, let's take a walk.'

I grab my coffee. Holly and Winter start chatting. The outside air is a welcome relief from the stuffiness of the office. Vince is saying little as we take the short walk across the parade square towards the gym.

Vince enters and puts his coffee down, takes off his jacket, and puts on the stereo that's stuck on BBC 6 Music.

Placebo's *You Don't Care About Us* is the song currently getting airtime.

'Come on, let's see if you've still got it,' Vince says as he locks the gym door. Not unusual if he doesn't want us to be overheard. He grabs a long bar and sets up the bench press.

He goes first at forty kilos. I spot him as he reps out.

'What's happening? We're alone, just me and you. Let me know what you know,' Vince says.

He's strong. Repping this weight and talking is child's play to him.

'You know what I know,' I say. 'We're waiting on them taking the Audi for a spin, then you'll take them out when they do the job. Holly and I are keeping the garage running, as you requested.'

He finishes his set. We swap and I do the same weight while he spots. The bar feels good, but where he's had his hands, the grip is wet.

Something is troubling him. I finish quickly. Vince ups the weight. He passes me another twenty-kilo plate, puts the same amount on his side and gets down under the bar.

'Don't fuck with me, Sam. I know you haven't brought everything up. You forget I've done the role you're in. What did you do to the tracker in the Audi? Come clean, or we're going to have a problem,' he says.

He cleans the bar off the stand and starts pushing his set out. We don't talk during his set.

He's trying to psych me out. He can't know anything, or he's holding his cards close to his chest. I put a marker on the PNC for the Mini's registration. If seen, or stopped, the officer is to contact me with the circumstances. I've heard nothing yet and I'll manage that easily if I'm contacted. I've been careful, very careful. There's been no surveillance team behind me. Of that, I'm certain. My phone is clean of calls in and out and no text messages either. I'm meticulous in my phone tradecraft. The phone he contacts me on is the work one I never use to call out.

I delegate to Holly to contact him and Winter. He's had no time to examine the Audi, either. He must be bluffing. Those covert kits are known to fail. I take the bar as he finishes the set and get under. I lie back and get comfy. He's sweating more now; the wet patch on the bench permeates my T-shirt.

I sit up and take my T-shirt off, laying it back on the bench.

I see Vince wince as he notes the scarring on my back and the ink that adorns my skin. My medals of honour. I'm pumped now. He needs the message I'm not to be toyed with. I won't react to his mind games.

I'm the soldier. I'll take part in his battle, but won't take any shit. I grip the bar and start pressing.

Vince leans over me. A bead of sweat drops from his forehead and hits my nose. I push through. The weight doesn't faze me. I live with worse discomfort.

I go to replace the bar, but Vince prevents me. My arms are locked out. Fatigue setting in.

'You either tell me what you're up to or I drop this bar on your smug fucking face,' he says.

He's serious. There's no play in his tone of voice. It's pure venom. I've riled him enough that he'd be willing to see me injured. He's chosen a good place. Any injury could be attributed to an accident in the gym. I'm not done yet though.

'You're full of shit,' I say. 'Always have been. Go on, do it! Mash me up. Grab the fucking bar, raise it up, and drop it on my nose.' My eyes are locked on his. My breathing's steady and strong.

'Smash my face to oblivion, Vince, because that's what you really want, isn't it? To see me removed from your operation. I know you think I'm a disgrace to the service, a ticking time bomb that no one desires to defuse. Tracking devices fail all the time. You know it as well as I do. You're fishing for dirt, just like Winter, but you're dipping your line in the wrong pond, Vince.'

He grabs the bar and pulls it back onto the safety stands. I sit up. Vince grabs his coat and exits the gym, leaving the door open. The only sound is coming from the stereo. Winter has got to him and he's getting paranoid. He was a hot-headed DC. Like most of us, he took no shit on the street and got the job done. He's got other ambitions now, and he doesn't want me messing them up.

Promotion is his target. He's chasing the higher lump sum and pension. It may not be my wish, but I like Vince. I have a lot of time for his old-school approach to delivering a message. Today was a warning shot, nothing more. He knows I'll do fuck all about it. I won't go to Winter complaining of overbearing conduct.

What happens in the gym stays in the gym. I need to give him something if I'm to keep him off my back.

I pick up my work phone and dial his number.

'Get what's left of your team and plot up around the Taverna in Green Lanes. I'll be there in an hour. Clock who goes in and out. I don't know if it will help.'

The sound of his breathing dominates the line.

'Don't be late,' he says and hangs up.

Now I've fed the lion, I hope it's enough to keep him satisfied.

24

Nines was easier to convince to meet at the snooker hall than I expected. He was already there. He'd called on the Turkish mafia too. According to Nines, the Turks wanted to meet me again. Build trust, he said.

I spend a couple of hours with Nines before using the fire exit at the rear of the restaurant to leave. Vince's team are covering the front. The longer Vince thinks I'm stuck in that club, partying, the better. The cab journey to Lambeth is easy. Now the Mini is gone, Little Chris has parked my latest car somewhere and left the keys under the front wheel arch.

Tonight is about getting things in order. My order. Little Chris has done well. I go to the road he told me it was in, and find a Ford Focus ST where he said it would be.

* * *

The drive across Blackfriars Bridge is smooth. Street lamps reflect off the polished black bonnet as dusk descends. Every so often the blue from a police light bounces back as a marked car flashes by. Vince hasn't made contact.

He's either stood his surveillance team down or he's carrying on until he hears from me.

I park away from my estate and walk to the flat.

I take the lift to my floor and exit right towards the landing. My neighbours are back. I noticed the blacked-out Range Rover in a parking bay with a hooded youth hanging around it as protection. My flat door is open. Russian voices coming from inside.

There are no goons on the landing. I have two choices: leave or face what's inside. I step in. Three heavies are sitting playing cards. I can hear wailing coming from the bedroom. These aren't sounds of pleasure.

'What the fuck are you doing in my flat?' I say.

A moustachioed heavy is the first to break concentration from his hand of cards and look up. He stands. His burly frame is imposing.

'This is no longer your flat, you are evicted. It is ours now.'

The other two turn around and stare in my direction.

'I'll need my clothes.'

I make for the bedroom door, but Mr Moustache stops me. 'It isn't the right time,' he says.

I assess the situation and agree. It isn't the right time, not tonight, at least.

'Okay,' I say. 'While you're here, I'm interested in having Olivia again? How much?'

There's conversation in Russian, heads are shaking.

'We don't have any Olivia, now go,' one of them replies.

'She's got blonde dyed hair, about twenty. I'll pay good money.' I direct my reply to them all.

None of them respond. The noises from the bedroom are increasing. I'm torn, I'm trying my best to establish if she's alive – she could be behind that door, but it could be someone else. I'm in no position to take the risk finding out. Finally, I get a response.

'How much you pay?' Mr Moustache says, his eyes wide with curiosity.

'Thousand, cash. I'll want her all day for that money though.' My eyes meet his, he locks on as he assesses my reply.

'How would a grease monkey like you get that kind of cash?' He's right of course.

'Don't you be concerned about my business. Do we have a deal, yes, or no?'

He turns to his other teammates none of whom are smiling.

'We do not. Go before I break your body into many pieces. I am a busy man.' Mr Moustache moves forward. He means what he says as he produces my own baseball bat from behind his tree-trunk-sized thigh. I bring my arms up in a sign of surrender and back out of the door of my own home.

I will return, but not tonight. Tonight is for research, and for that I need another car. The youth by the Range Rover approaches as I get closer to the vehicle.

'Get the fuck away from the car, man, or I'll skiv ya.' He displays his intention in the form of a filleting knife, the blade of which glints in the overhead lamp.

'I need this car for an hour, then I'll bring it back. You've got the keys, right?' It's a long shot, but it would be good to know all the same.

The kid's eyes are shifty. He has the keys but he's not going to give them up to me just yet. 'Look, bruv, just fuck off.' He's moving forward as he speaks.

'What price, for the ride, for an hour? C'mon, Nines will reference me. He knows I'll bring the motor back, untouched. The foreign bodies will never know anything. What do you say?'

The kid's not dismissing the idea now I've dropped Nines' name into the conversation.

'You know Nines?' he says.

'I do.'

'Look, man, I'd say yeah as I need the dough, but those Russian guys don't fuck about. If they see the motor gone, I'm a dead man.' The knife is away now. The kid takes out a rollup and sparks up.

'Forty-five minutes tops. I'll have it back here, safe and sound. They'll never know it's gone. There's a hundred cash for you.'

The kid starts listening.

'You'll deffo bring it back? I know Nines and I know your flat, so you better be sweet on this.'

'If I don't bring it back in time, I'll pay you five hundred for your trouble.'

'Deal.' The kid produces the keys and I hand over four twenties wrapped in a folded twenty. He sees the notes and nods.

I get in the car and the kid's gone. It's a manual transmission. My leg will survive operating the clutch for the short trip it's needed for. The interior's clean. I engage the first gear and head towards my own vehicle. The engine's good, I've time on my side. I park alongside the Ford and place a crowbar I'd asked Little Chris to leave in the new car into the Range Rover.

I check my watch: ten minutes have elapsed. Night has descended into the early hours. Stragglers from parties and minicab drivers are the main people on the street.

I remind myself that I'm entitled to be here, unloading the contents of one car into another – it's nothing unusual by London standards.

I get back in the Range Rover and drive away. I keep checking my mirrors, pulling over regularly, letting traffic pass. Then I see the service station Nines took me to when we first dispensed with the cash. There are very few people about and the forecourt's deserted. A light wind has started flicking up litter and road dust.

I look around and check the time. I've used half of my forty-five minutes' allowance. Time to go to work. I trace the alarm cable and cut it before I jam the crowbar in the side of the cash machine and create a gap. I check the area again. There's no one in the main garage. The attendant must be out back, until summoned. I insert more pressure. The front pops off, exposing the cash trays. The machine's been rigged to allow easy access to them. Word must be out the machine is off limits to rob. I grab the cash trays, bung them in the Range Rover and leave.

Time is on my side. I arrive back at my car and put everything into the Ford before taking the Range Rover back to the estate. With three minutes to spare I draw up and park. I kill the lights and the engine ticks down from idle to off.

There's a tap on the window. The kid's alongside, furtive, and anxious. I get out and throw him the keys and his face changes to one of relief.

'Thank fuck you're back, man. I thought you'd done one. What did you need it for anyways?'

'Loose lips sink ships. I may need to use her again.'

The kid agrees. I hand him another wad of cash and he takes it.

'Mention a word to anyone and I'll cut your fucking tongue out,' I say. He nods.

I walk away from the estate. Once I'm sufficiently clear, I get a cab close to where the Ford is parked. I get dropped three streets away and walk. I get in the car, then text Vince.

Leaving soon. All good.

He replies.

Okay I'll stand the team down.

I engage the engine and U-turn towards the A406 and back to my industrial facility.

25

I finish counting the cash. Thirty thousand pounds to be exact. I learnt at the club that the Turks were due to collect it tonight and take it to another holding point – a gambling joint they run from a house. They like to spread the cash around, so it isn't all in one place. If they're stopped by police, they'll produce the crypto receipt. It won't show any amount, just a code.

I place the money in the safe and secure the door, then drive back to the Hendon office.

Vince sent a text out earlier for us to stand down until 2 p.m.

His logic is that the targets were partying at the snooker club and had not left the venue until the early hours, according to a static camera feed that recorded the entrance from the observation van. It was cheaper than keeping his team on all night, and he only wanted to identify any other associates of Nines and Sugar.

I'm aware it won't have recorded me leaving. If I'm asked, I'll confess to using a rear exit. Nothing you can do when a target insists you leave by it.

At the office, my Nines phone rings.

'We've got a problem,' he says. 'Someone screwed the cash machine. The attendant didn't see nothing. I've had word the Russians' Range Rover was seen around there, but Shanks, who minds it, says it never left his sight. This ain't good. The Turks are spitting blood, reckoning the Russians robbed them. There'll be a war.'

I begin to warm to Shanks but recognise he may become a liability. I doubt it, though. He won't be keen to get implicated in a money rip-off where Nines, the Turks, and a firm of Russians are concerned. Not if he values his life.

'Meet me at the garages,' Nines continues. 'We need to get that money back.' He cuts the line.

I call Vince.

'Nines just called me to the garage. Sounds like he intends to roll.'

'I'll get the team ramped up. Don't leave until I tell you we're good to go. I'll message you some shit about car repairs. That'll be the message that we're in position.' Vince hangs up.

I grab my coat and the keys to my car. The Tiger Trap gate to our site shuts me in and the lead gate opens to Aerodrome Road.

I take a right and head towards Brent Cross to pick up the North Circular. Holly calls. She'll be in the vicinity should I need her. That's probably Vince's idea. He won't want to freak this lot out if they intend to roll on to a job. I can't say I blame him.

I dump the Ford and get a bus. Nines is with Sugar, both are on foot, and sitting on the tyre pile as I approach the garage.

'Where have you been?' Nines says.

'Never you mind. Let's get inside.' I unlock the main garage door and lift it; we all duck in. I press a red button on the wall and the doors close. I flick on a socket that powers an inspection lamp. This activates an additional recorder. I hope it's working.

Nines isn't happy. He has a 9mm pistol pointing at my face motioning me towards the inspection pit that's dug out of the floor.

'Get in.'

I do as he says.

He takes a can of petrol and places it next to him at the pit edge. This isn't going as I'd envisaged.

'I'm guessing from all this I've done something to upset you?' I say.

Nines breathes heavily through his nose weighing the pistol in his hands. He looks high.

'I have a bug I can't get shot of. That bug's you. You were the only one who knew what we dropped off the other night, and that it was getting collected today. Then it goes and gets turned over. All very convenient, don't you think? My money's on you unless you can convince me otherwise. If you don't, you and this garage are going up in flames.'

Sugar is picking up the petrol container. He's not wearing gloves. Neither of them are.

They're either bluffing or sure that they're invincible. I'm going with the first but need a way out that's convincing.

'Why would I rock up here if I'd done you? I'd be an idiot. Whoever's done it is crazy or some punk opportunist who got lucky. Now you can torch me all you like, but if you do, then know this, you've got the wrong man. That's not my style. I was with you in the pool club, or has your drug-addled brain forgotten that?' I wait to see if either of them give a shit or whether they'll just waste me.

Nines' breathing becomes more regular. He's looking quizzical as he thinks back to us being at the pool club. They were both wasted by the time I left, and they know it. How do I know? The crushed tablets of morphine I'd slipped in their drinks were taking effect.

He motions to Sugar who offers a hand. I brush myself down at the pit edge, glad I never brought the Sig pistol from Mike's safe, as I'd have blown the wiry little fuck away. But this is work, and it's time to get on with it.

'Back to work, I guess,' I say.

I investigate the engine of one of the stooge cars, clipping the inspection light to the underside of the bonnet to add to the illusion of knowledge. Nines passes the gun to Sugar, who stuffs it in his waistband and pulls his hoody down at the back.

'We're out on a recce tonight,' he says. 'Have the Audi ready. If the opportunity's there we'll take it.' Nines scans the garage as he speaks.

'Do want me to drive?' I ask.

'Yeah.'

'I need to know what the job could be. It helps me prep, mentally,' I say.

Nines tilts his head, releasing tension in his neck.

'We take out cash-in-transit vans. When I say take out, I mean obliterate them. Your job is to get us close to the van and out. You'll be on top of the action – not parked up, waiting for us to return. Fuck up or get the Old Bill involved, and you're a dead man. I ain't doing more time. This could be our last hit before we lie low for a while. We've been all over the news. The cops will be sniffing around, and we don't want them catching our scent. The Turks want their cut and so do the Russians. I'm down thirty grand and most of that goes to the other two firms.' Nines takes a breath, then continues.

'Meet us in West Hendon Broadway near the Jewish school tonight at eight. It's the old place that used to house the Operation Trident lot back in the day. If you're late, your cut gets cut, so don't mess up.' Nines gestures to Sugar, and they leave via the emergency exit.

I smile and wink for the benefit of the covert camera that's in the engine compartment of the car we were huddled around. I go to the wall socket and flick the recording device off. My work here is done.

26

'Gather round, gather round.' Vince is on top form and keen to despatch his troops – a band of detectives all armed and keen to go. They know Nines is in no position to lie low. He still owes money despite his loss. Vince confirms call signs, and runs through the targets and expectations.

Why am I here? For his team to recognise the person they're not to shoot.

The squad leave to re-group by their vehicles and check over the equipment one last time before rolling out towards the target area. Radio checks commence, the vibe is positive. Vince pulls me to one side.

'Winter wants you wired for this outing,' he says, handing me a covert body-worn recording kit.

It's uncomfortable, cumbersome, and could lead to my death if discovered.

'No way. I'm not wearing that. Not tonight. You've seen the footage from the garage earlier. They mean business. It's too risky.'

'For fuck's sake, you've been in worse situations wired, so use your skill, and you'll be fine.'

"Cross your fingers and hope" was not the reassurance I was looking for.

Winter strides in, mobile phone at her ear.

'Yes … I'll update with any developments, Commander.' She ends the call.

'Batford,' she says, 'get the wire on, and quit moaning. We've not got much time.'

She then turns to Vince. 'That was Commander Barnes. The commissioner's taking an interest in your operation. There's nervousness about the cash vans from the drivers' union. Threats of strike action if this gang isn't taken out. If this doesn't happen tonight, then we may have to go with what we've got.'

This gets Vince riled.

I take the covert set I have no intention of wearing.

'That's a joke, Klara, and you know it. Sam was shrewd earlier, and they trust him enough to drive. I know resources are tight, but we have an opportunity to bang this lot up for a long time if we take them out during an armed robbery. You must see that?' Vince says.

'Don't shoot the messenger, Vince. I'll do what I can, but take this as a heads-up,' says Winter. 'Money talks, especially where the banks are concerned and cash flow is interrupted. Without these cash vans, businesses suffer, and that's not good for our reputation as protectors either. What will Holly's role be?'

'She'll be my cover officer while I'm out,' I say, before either of them has any other stupid ideas.

Winter nods. 'Very good. I'll be monitoring the radio from the covert control room. Don't let me down, gentlemen.'

With her motivational speech complete, Winter grabs her bag and leaves. Vince has a look of resignation, not at the work but at his position with Winter. He's not used to such close supervision. His own superintendent just used to let him crack on, as did his DCI. Winter is a rare breed and one that needs tethering. Problem is, she has a knack of shaking the rope loose.

I take advantage of this moment to depart.

'I'm on the phone. I'll call when I'm out,' I say.

'Put the wire on!' Vince says.

I hold it up, so he sees I have it. I get my phones from the secure cabinet outside the office door and switch them on. No messages. I lock the covert kit away and take the key. The evening's looking good, no rain forecast, and there's the faintest glimmer of stars despite the smog of artificial light that prevents decent viewing.

I ponder what I'll do with the thirty grand in the industrial site safe. Truth is, I don't need it. I needed Nines to get shaken up. I know what Mike would do. Reinvest it in another car or casino. I'm not Mike, but it's become apparent that much of his ethos has rubbed off, despite my resistance to warp into his world of excess and glamour.

I own his criminal empire and can think of nothing worse. Yes, I'm damaged. Damaged beyond repair. My body destroyed through a bullet, morphine, and a history of physical abuse. On the plus side, I have a private pension, courtesy of my criminal mind.

I think of the soldier in the park, lost and destitute despite his service to this country. And Olivia, another soul abused for criminal gain and extortion.

I'm done with maudlin. DS Batford has gone. Welcome back, Sky.

27

The Audi grips the road. The low-profile tyres, blacked-out windows, and gunmetal-grey exterior give it a menacing look. This is a cop's dream stop: three armed robbers on a drive out.

Holloway Road turns into Archway Road. I slow down for the speed camera as we approach the infamous bridge where I'd seen the girl jump to her death. Scaffolding encases the pub. Steel props are in place to maintain what's left of the ceiling and exterior structure. Nines and Sugar are chilling, smoking dope, moving their heads to the stereo that's pumping out grime.

The music is doing my head in, but it's my job to get them where they need to be. I check my external mirrors. I see a motorbike that could be the surveillance rider. I'm unsure. The more relaxed I am, the better. I'll know if I need to make the break.

'What's up with you? You ain't saying shit?' Sugar says from the back seat.

No one wants to ride shotgun tonight, which is a good thing. I hate passengers. More so when they're too close.

'Let's just say being placed in a pit, and threatened with being torched, has dulled my desire to make small talk,' I say, glancing in the rearview mirror. The whites of Nines' eyes look back from the dark void.

'I was messing with you, man. You know that. Thing is, that money was meant for your neighbours and they ain't happy. I have a new shipment coming and they want first pick,' Nines says.

This is news to me. 'You ship girls for the Russians?' I say.

'Nah, not exactly.' Nines looks out of his blacked-out window. 'I dabble in all sorts: drugs, guns, and women being my main commodities. They've been struggling after a container got searched. The girls got discovered along with a batch of guns. Thankfully, the load was split. The Skorpion machine pistols and explosive for the van doors wasn't taken. The Russians don't like it when shipments of guns don't come through. Girls ain't a problem... Go right, go right!'

I swing the car as directed and cruise towards Muswell Hill Broadway. I stay quiet in the hope Nines will continue talking.

He leans forward. 'We're nearly there,' he says. 'Cruise these streets, make sure we're alone.' Nines is looking to flush police out of any hiding spots.

I look at the road ahead. Buses are parked on the roundabout. They provide good cover as I drive around and double back. I'm conscious of not looking for surveillance or doing anything drastic to lose them. That wouldn't be wise at this stage of the game. If this lot gets nicked, then so be it. I'll have only gained the thirty grand and a course in basic vehicle mechanics.

Right now, I can live with those gains. I'm tired and need a break from the constant watch I feel under from outside and within. I'm sick of the music too, and the craving for a spliff is doing my head in.

'Can't we have something else on other than this shit?' I say.

Nines is concentrating on what's happening out of the window. I see why. Outside the Marks & Spencer store is a cash van that's just pulled up. No one's out yet.

'Spin around,' Nines says.

Sugar's looking into a bag by his feet. He hands Nines a balaclava. I double back from the roundabout and park on the opposite side, facing towards Highgate.

Nines looks out the rear window. 'Don't kill the engine,' he demands.

I leave it running. I'm hoping Vince's team will be ready to strike. Then I see two of Vince's team out on foot.

There's a pensive silence. Sugar brings out a Skorpion automatic and lays it across his lap like a bride rests her bouquet in a wedding car. Their stoicism astounds me. I've been in many situations, both armed and unarmed, and nerves always play a part before the hit, yet these two make it look like they're out shopping.

'Okay, one guard out, into the shop, carrying a box. Get ready, Sugar, get ready. Sky, when I say so, get close to the van. I'll deal with the guard, get the box, and throw it in the back, then we're away,' Nines says.

So much for a recce.

Nines has the 9mm on his lap. They've both got balaclavas over their faces. Sugar throws me one and I put it on. I keep checking mirrors and wait for the shout. I'll need to get to the other side smoothly, without alerting the guard carrying the cash. I switch the radio off and give the accelerator a blip. The red needle goes up the dial.

The sliding door to the shop opens. A customer enters. The edge of the box emerges with the helmet of the guard.

'Floor it, floor it!' Nines screams.

I engage drive and sweep the Audi over two lanes towards the van, the rear doors facing me. The guard turns in my direction. A yellow and blue stripe catches my attention. A marked police car comes over the brow of Muswell Hill roundabout and pulls towards the van. I wrench the steering wheel left and accelerate.

It's too late. The cop is switched on and figured out what was about to go down. Blue lights and two tones break our silence.

'What the fuck!' Nines yells as the force of our acceleration throws him back in his seat along with Sugar. They'd both had their hands on the door handles ready to bail out when I'd swung the Audi violently away.

The engine roars as I tear down Colney Hatch Lane towards the North Circular and East Finchley. The traffic's heavier now. I guide the Audi on the wrong side of the road forcing oncoming vehicles to move over. Red traffic lights mean nothing. The cop is keeping pace with me. Headlights and blue pulses flash in time with the two-tone siren.

'Keep down and let me do my job.' I shout at them both as they peer out from over the back headrests.

'They're getting closer,' Sugar shouts above the sound of the engine.

I'm close to the A406. Cars are moving over as they hear the sirens. I career past them. I look again, a bus has stalled the cop car. The officer has nowhere to move. His vision is limited to the back of the bus. I risk it and take the next left into a residential street where I see a garage block.

I pull in and kill the engine. 'Leave the shooters. Go, go.'

They don't need telling twice. They leave the guns but keep their gloves and balaclavas on. They climb the garage roof and are away. I wait and open the window, listening for more sirens approaching the area to assist with the search. There's nothing.

I check my watch. It's 2145 hours. I shove the guns into the concealed boot space, wait a further five minutes then leave.

28

There's a hum of chat as I approach the office door. I place my phones in the small locker cage and take out the covert recording kit before entering. Holly's here along with Vince and Winter, all sat around a meeting table. Holly looks up and smiles. I can't decide if it's a smile of welcome or a smile of nerves at what's to come. I join them in the remaining seat.

'Anything off the recording?' Winter says.

'Nothing. It was a fucking nightmare in the car. Too muffled.'

I leave that hanging as Winter takes off her Tom Ford reading glasses and rests the end of one arm in her mouth. She's pissed off. 'You never wore it, did you?' she says. 'You make my life and that of the ops team a living nightmare. If we weren't this far in with these players, I'd ditch you. Trust me, I have the power to do so.' She sits back in her chair and directs her gaze at Vince.

I say nothing. There's little point in entering a hole I'd struggle to climb out of while Winter keeps filling it with dirt.

'We'll talk after this meeting, Sam. What happened yesterday?' Vince says.

'They were ready to execute the blag, but a marked car pulled up at the wrong time. I took an operational decision to abort. To carry on would have been suicide for me and members of the public. They had a Skorpion automatic pistol and a handgun between them. I believe they would have shot anyone in their way.'

Vince is taking notes, as is Winter.

I continue. 'We were pursued. I evaded. Nines and Sugar made off. We spoke this morning. They want to link up again but haven't suggested a date or time yet. If you'd fixed the Audi's covert recording, you'd be able to verify my account. I take it your surveillance team wasn't behind us either.'

Vince stops writing. He shoots me a look I interpret as saying "shut the fuck up".

'I'll ignore that,' he says. 'Sam did provide intel of a pool table venue above the Taverna in Green Lanes that's being used by our targets. From surveillance, we've been able to identify a Turkish gang known to launder money. They also have Russian connections. One of them was inside when Nines was doing time – that's how they met. My instinct is telling me to put the last run down to bad luck. We roll again as soon as they call. They're up for it, Sam,' Vince says.

Vince looks to Winter for approval but is disappointed.

'Why? We can nick them all for conspiracy to rob and a host of connected offences. We also have control of the guns,' Winter says, expecting agreement. She'll be waiting a while.

'No way. We arrest now, and this lot will walk from court. I want them caught during a hit when they're out on the ground. We have the line facility. We'll know when it's happening,' Vince says.

'Results are what I need. Bodies in custody. If I have nothing soon, you'll do as I direct,' Winter says.

It's surprising how quick attitudes can change after a promotion. It wasn't that long ago she would have wanted the same result as Vince.

Meeting done. Vince and Winter stay behind to resolve their differences. Holly and I leave them to it.

Nines and Sugar will be on high alert. The next job must come off or they may start asking questions as to why they are getting disrupted. I'm the only major change. Toots has become an open missing-person report that will close when his body is found. I don't wish to go the same way.

'What's your plan? It's clear where they both think I fit in the job,' Holly says.

I feel for her. She hands me a coffee and we return to our own desks. I see a copy of the *Metro* on hers.

'Can I take a look?' I ask.

She hands it to me. On the front cover is the picture of the soldier I'd met in the park. I only know it's him by a picture of the fella wearing the medals he showed me from better days. Alongside it is a face that's a swollen mess of dark and yellow blotches. He's been mugged. His medals taken. There's an appeal for information.

'You look like you know him?' Holly says.

'I don't. But I don't like it when a soldier gets treated like that.' I hand her back the paper.

'Keep it, I'm done,' she says.

I pause and place it back on my desk, then turn on the computer. My Nines phone goes. I don't recognise the number. I get up and grab my jacket.

'Tell Vince and Winter I'll be in touch soon.' I show Holly the phone and she nods her understanding. Once I'm clear of the building, I answer it.

'Who's this?' I say.

'It's me.'

I recognise Nines' voice.

'Bit tight last night,' I say.

'I take it everything's back where it should be?'

'Everything's in place. What happens now?' I say.

'We go on Friday. I'll be in touch with details. This is my new number.' The line goes dead.

He's jumpy, that's for certain.

I have two days to fulfil other priorities before Friday. The line Vince had under surveillance is now lost. The guns bother me.

How Vince and Winter are justifying an armed intervention when we could seize the guns and arrest Nines and Sugar now is above my paygrade to understand.

29

Two days are left before the next heist. I hunker down in the Tesla I'd collected from the industrial site and prepare for my next move. I won't have long. This car is not known to the estate and will attract unwanted attention. I'd thought about using the Ford, but not for this outing. I can lose the Tesla but Little Chris expects the Ford back.

I called Winter to confirm what she said was true about the time we had left to bring these targets in. She is giving us until midnight on Friday. If Nines doesn't play, they're getting arrested for conspiracy to commit robbery and possession of firearms. This evening, I've decided to conduct my own investigation on behalf of Olivia.

I use the Tesla's in-car touch screen and surf the web for a local curry delivery. Using a burner phone to dial it in, I arrange one, and wait.

A short while passes before I hear the hum of a moped engine. The erratic weaving from a single headlight catches my eye in the rearview mirror.

I get out of the car. The delivery guy approaches dressed in a bland gilet jacket with the "Curry in a Hurry" logo embroidered on it. He sees me and stops. He doesn't like delivering in this area. He's shifty and just wants to get out with the money as fast as possible. His eyes glance back at his moped to ensure he's not being robbed. He removes his crash helmet and puts on a company cap. I pay the rider for the meal, he hands over a brown bag and he's gone.

I lock the car and set off in the direction of my old block. The weight of the Sig pistol in my waistband provides a reassuring comfort.

The door to my flat is shut. Lights are on inside. There's a mix of male voices coming from within, along with music. There are no sentries on the landing. I bash on the door. A shadow appears in the small, frosted glass window at the front. The door opens. A Russian who looks as though he could wrestle a bear blocks the entrance.

'What do you want? You have the wrong address.' He's straight to the point.

'No one order curry?' I say.

'I told you, wrong address. What is it anyway?' The smell is tempting him.

'House special. All the meats and more.'

'Bring it in. Shame to waste it.' He opens the door fully.

Down the hall are two more heavies. Olivia is laid on the sofa, wasted. Bottles of vodka are half empty.

'Leave it on the table and go,' the Russian says.

'I need paying,' I say.

'Why the hell did you let him in?' The heavy from the hall recognises me.

I whip the Sig from my waistband.

My first shot enters the mouth of the goon who answered the door. The bullet exits his head along with half his skull. The heavy who recognised me reaches behind him. He gets the same treatment. Olivia is rousing now. Thanks to the silencer, there's little noise. The music blares, masking the sound of bodies hitting the deck.

The last man freezes, dropping to his knees, weeping like a child at the hands of a brutal parent.

I'm numb to his pleas for clemency.

Grabbing a fist of hair, I turn his face towards Olivia who's wearily raising her head in our direction. Her eyes are trying to open, but she's so out of it she can't see.

'This is your doing,' I say. 'Her life is fucked up because of men like you. I wreck lives too. I'm not a mercenary or gun for hire. I'm a detective sergeant.'

His eyes search mine, as he takes in what I'm telling him.

'As your friend said, I'm foolish. Foolish for coming here, showing my face, and admitting I'm a cop. I have no backup,' I say.

He looks up at me then turns to Olivia.

I've had enough.

'We're done,' I say, shooting the Russian in the forehead.

The scene will look like a mob execution. Leaving Olivia where she is, I put on one of the Russian's coats, grab the curry, and depart.

Back in the car, I request an ambulance for Olivia. My work is done. She won't remember a thing given the state she was in. She'll be taken to hospital, where she'll get help. The Russian's coat I'll ditch in my industrial site bin.

I need to clean up. There'll be traces of blood on me. You don't make that kind of mess and walk away as virgin as you came in. I look at the curry on the floor of the car and wonder whether it will microwave.

I hate seeing food go to waste.

I input my destination to the industrial site and the car sets the quickest route. It's not long before I'm back at the site parking the Tesla in its charging bay. I let the driver's door rise to open, get out, and plug it in to charge. The only thing I need now is the curry and a beer. The gun, I leave out to clean. I left bullet casings at the scene, but that was intentional.

Along with the Russians' hardware, it will fit the scene well. They carry the same weapon I executed them with. Hopefully the police will focus on finding a vodka-fuelled disgruntled card player pissed at losing a hand. My gun won't be around for much longer.

30

Winter has requested an urgent meeting. Vince, Holly, and I gather in a meeting room at New Scotland Yard that could accommodate more than the three of us.

News of a gangland execution is out.

I've done society a service, that's the way I see it. I won't deny it felt good. Eradicating parasites is always rewarding work.

I've viewed the computer-aided dispatch reference to the scene. The CAD reference hasn't been set to restricted access yet, an oversight I'm thankful for. It shows the London Ambulance Service attended, and drove a female to an unidentified hospital. She's under armed guard and remains in a stable condition. Fears of a return hit are high. The senior investigating officer will be playing safe.

The murder team will explore why she wasn't shot. One theory will be the shooter was disturbed or that she couldn't witness anything due to her condition, so she was spared. The latter is weak, but relevant. The ambulance is said to have been called in by an unidentified male voice. The murder team won't be able to follow that up, unless I've been picked up on camera or the curry delivery guy sticks his hand up and provides a photo-fit of me. I doubt he'll remember me. It was dark and I had my hood up. I'm pleased Olivia's safe.

The door opens and Commander Barnes enters along with Winter. This isn't good. Barnes is head of specialist operations and has the ultimate say in any undercover operation. Vince shuffles in his seat as Barnes and Winter settle at one end of the table along with the commander's PA. Vince has brought a detective sergeant from his team.

Nines was also up early. He phoned, wanting to meet over at Finsbury Park. I put him off. He wasn't happy. It would appear I'm upsetting everyone.

Barnes opens the meeting. 'As you're all aware, there was a triple murder at the covert flat last night. We're relieved DS Batford was no longer living there.' She turns to me and smiles. Not what I expected.

'Detective Superintendent Winter had briefed me as to the reasons the address was no longer safe. Now it's a murder scene, it would appear the risk assessment was accurate. Since the attacks in Salisbury, the Counter Terrorism unit are taking on all serious crime where a Russian national is implicated. They'll need your prints and DNA to eliminate you from the scene, Sam. I've briefed my colleague at SO15 as to your role in this operation and your links to the flat. No one is suggesting your involvement. It's for elimination purposes only.'

A warm glow flushes through my body. SO15 is Counter Terrorism Command. They're heavily resourced and don't tread lightly.

'Of course, ma'am. A shame it's been detrimental to our investigation,' I say.

'Not at all. In fact, it's added value to it. Klara?' The commander finishes.

Winter smooths her skirt, picks up a folder, and hands out copies marked "For our eyes only, not to leave the room".

'Vince's intelligence unit has contacted SO15,' Winter says. 'They've shared intelligence on the murder victims. There's a connection with Nines and his associates. Nines is part of a people-trafficking network that supplies drugs to the Russian syndicate. Sources have been hearing that Nines is seeking revenge for the attacks and offering a street reward should anyone find out who was responsible. His cash flow is diminished. Police are all over the estate conducting high-visibility reassurance patrols, which makes his daily activities harder. Word is, he owes money to the Russians and is looking to do another robbery so he can pay them back.' Winter pauses. She looks up and sees we're all attentive.

I wonder why Nines would pay back a debt when all the men are dead.

Winter continues, almost as if reading my mind. 'Intelligence from SO15 suggests the head of the Russian syndicate wasn't present at the shooting. This gives us another headache. What if our assassin is seeking the head of the operation and won't stop killing until they're found? Early investigative leads show two of the victims were clean shots to the head. The last one was executed at close range. A female was found alive at the scene. She was taken to the Whittington Hospital. She was unconscious on arrival and hasn't spoken yet. There's an armed post in place to make sure she's safe. She's obviously a potential witness. It may be the assassin was disturbed and therefore may return to finish what he or she started. Intelligence suggests she's from a consortium of young girls brought over to use as drug mules and for sexual exploitation through prostitution. If there's no terrorist connection, then the enquiry will be handed back to a murder team at Hendon.'

'So where does that leave me and my team?' Vince asks.

The commander takes over. 'Continue being proactive. Your enquiry is separate to that of SO15. The SIO for SO15 will be applying for intrusive surveillance. This includes our targets. He has agreed to share any intel on imminent armed robberies. DS Batford, as the shooting took place in the flat you were living in, you will be placed under twenty-four-hour surveillance until this operation is concluded. It will be part of conduct authorisation. I expect it to be adhered to, no excuses.'

'Ma'am, I don't have the staff to provide cover for DS Batford. All my resources are on the targets,' Vince says.

'I'm aware of that. Detective Superintendent Winter has acquired the services of her old team from the National Crime Agency to assist at this crucial stage of the operation. It's a team who know you, DS Batford, and I'm sure you'll cooperate with them.' The sarcasm in her voice is not disguised.

'Without question, ma'am. I appreciate the lengths you're going to, to ensure my safety,' I lie.

The commander's expression shows her ambivalence towards me. She knows I'm the closest thing to Nines they have. Nines is no fool. He's revealed a different number to me just today. I'm trusted. My phone vibrates. It's a text from him.

Meet at the Taverna in an hour.

I don't respond. I need to appear to be playing by the rules with the commander, especially now SO15 are involved.

'That was Nines. He's dropping the number I gave to Vince. I'm to meet him in an hour at the snooker club. Hopefully he'll pass me a new line,' I say.

'That will save SO15 work. Thank you, Sam,' the commander says.

'I need to leave,' I say, getting up.

'You can't leave. The NCA team aren't ready,' Winter says.

Vince hangs his head in his hands. He knows if I don't go, the job could be lost, the contact dropped, and Nines would move on.

'I'll get my team over to the restaurant,' Vince cuts in quickly.

The commander looks at Winter. 'I'll leave this with you, Klara. You're aware of my instructions. Meeting's over.' With that, Barnes gets up and leaves, her PA trailing behind her.

'Make contact when you get there and when you leave,' Winter says to me.

I look to Vince, then exit the room. I need to get to Embankment where I can hail a cab.

31

Rain slaps me in the face as I exit the tube at Turnpike Lane. Puddles have become rivulets. I stay away from the kerb and walk towards the restaurant.

A bus draws up and I get on. I glance through the window. Vince is out. I know this because he's phoning me. I answer.

'Where in the fuck are you going?' he says.

I cup the mouthpiece to muffle my voice. 'Get the surveillance in the car behind off me, and I'll return.'

'Fuck's sake, your call,' Vince says and hangs up.

The car behind the bus turns left. I get off at the next stop, walk back, and into the restaurant.

I'm not searched, just waved upstairs by the door jammer as he resumes his post.

There's a heavy atmosphere.

'Who's died?' I say to Nines who's sat at the bar.

'You are telling me you ain't heard about the shit that went down at your place last night?' Nines says.

I help myself to a beer behind the bar.

'I haven't been there for days. I was kicked out by my neighbours. Didn't fancy my chances of getting the place back. I've been dossing at the garage,' I say.

I take a swig of warm Corona, no lime. Nines looks at Sugar. Sugar shrugs in a way I take to mean I sound legit.

'We've got some major shit going down on the manor. Three of my associates got gunned down in your flat last night. I'm getting heat from the Turks and the Russians' boss. I want to know where you were.'

He's not convinced with my story. I like him.

'I was at the garage, like I said. I took the eviction on the chin. I was going to ask you to put a word in for me as you control the estate, but I was fine.'

A blade appears from inside his sleeve. He's lost his mind.

'I should never have got you involved in my business,' Nines says. 'Ever since you turned up, the vibe has gone to shit! It was all running well until you moved in.' He lunges with the blade.

The knife sweeps under my raised right arm. I take hold of his wrist in my left hand and invert it towards his throat.

I'm stronger than him. He's on his knees and the blade tips his Adam's apple.

'Tell Sugar to stay where he is,' I say coldly, 'or I'll run you through and then kill him.'

Sugar doesn't need telling. He must remember the last time I had a weapon in the flat. Nines spits in my face. I bend his wrist further back towards his forearm and he drops the knife. I put my left foot on the blade. No chance of me being cut there. I release his wrist. He stands up. I bend down and pick up the knife.

'If you want me to work with you then you cut this shit out and focus on who's looking to take over your turf. For the record, I'm not interested. I make what I make and take what I take. You won't be out of pocket though, that's not my style. You're getting paranoid. Either our job is on, or I walk, and put all this down to experience. I can go anywhere a car needs fixing.' I finish the beer and wipe my mouth on the sleeve of my jacket.

'All right, all right,' Nine says, dusting himself off. 'This hit has fucked me up. I owe the Russians a shit load of cash. Whoever took them out won't stop there. They'll want me too. A debt's a debt, whoever takes on the business. Five-Oh are all over the estate, so takings are down on the street and I ain't got ready access to cash. The cash I take goes to the Russians. I'm not starting a war with no one to gain a street or two to deal from. We were unlucky the other night. I've got a man on the inside who sorts the cash runs. Friday is a big collection day. That's when we hit a van. I ain't telling you when or where. Too many people are talking. I can't be taking risks no more. I called you here to see if you'd turn up and how you'd react. I'm happy if you are?'

I tell him I'm cool with everything.

Sugar leans over the bar and reaches behind.

I grip the knife, and hold it close.

He brings out a box and opens it. In it are three pay-as-you-go mobile phones, all new and sealed.

'Take one,' Nines says. 'Get it charged up. I'll call on Friday at midday. Don't turn it on till then. I'll let you know where to meet. Bring the Audi. I can't fuck about with another motor. It's too late for a respray and new plates. Now, let's relax before my next meeting.'

Nines picks up a landline from behind the counter. Bar staff appear and the pool area opens. He goes to a different room with a group of Turks who've come up with the bar staff. His next meeting is under way. I need to relax. It's game on.

32

I leave the Taverna worse for wear. As I head towards Finsbury Park, I feel as though I'm being tailed. The sense turns to reality when a hand grips my shoulder. I swing round and there's Vince. He escorts me off the street into the back of his nondescript car and heads off.

'You're wasted. What happened?' Vince says. He turns right to an area the locals call the "Harringay Ladder" because of the way the streets connect.

'I was threatened with a blade. Calmed it all down and kept the job alive. It's a goer. Day after tomorrow. No time or place, but they want me to drive. They'll contact me at the garage. I didn't get another number from Nines. Hopefully the anti-terrorist lot will establish one and let us know. I had to party as was expected by the crew.'

I lie across the back. I can't give Vince the number I have for Nines or tell him about the new phone. I have my own safety to consider. Nines is on edge. The phone and strict instructions could all be a test to flush me out.

'Good.' All I hear is the change in engine revs as Vince dances through the gears.

'I need to be at the garage. They want to use the car on Friday,' I say.

Vince checks his rearview mirror. I smile at him as I pull up my hood and despite the damp fabric I enjoy how it warms up against my head.

'I'm taking a trip to Argos and getting you a camp bed,' he says. 'You'll need some comfort at the garage now you've no flat.' He smiles at me through the mirror – his way of letting me know that he understands how I operate.

I don't question him. Let him think what he likes. If he knew how I'd been operating, he'd be taking me into custody, not shopping.

He carries on. 'Ballistics came back with an initial report from the shootings. All 9mm, non-attributable shells. No link to any similar ammo being found at a crime scene. SO15 are looking to hand it back to the murder team. There's no link to terrorism. Good job you weren't staying there. Where were you staying?'

'At the garage. I was alone. Never had any meet during the time that would warrant recording, so the cameras were off,' I say.

'Oi, it was just a question of welfare, nothing more. I need to know where you are, Sam, in case it all comes on top. You heard the commander. You could have stayed at mine, you know?'

'I don't think Lydia and the kids would appreciate me being there,' I say.

Vince doesn't reply and turns towards Hornsey.

'I could do with something to eat. I'm starving,' I say.

'Yeah, let's sort that out. We'll get away from this area though. I know a good place,' Vince says.

I lie back and try to sleep but the potholes and undulation of the roads prevents it.

33

I wake up on a camp bed in the garage cocooned in a sleeping bag. There's someone in the kitchen. I look below the zip line of the bag. I'm fully clothed. A half bottle of Grants lies empty on the floor alongside an empty strip of morphine.

A rumble of boiling water hits its peak followed by a click. It must be Holly. Despite the hangover from whisky and prescription opiates, I feel okay. Holly comes through, hands me a mug, and sits in a chair.

'Vince was in two minds whether to call Occupational Health. I persuaded him I'd watch over you. You're a fitful sleeper, that's for sure,' Holly says.

I sit up and swing my legs around in the sleeping bag.

'Where did you sleep?' I say. There's nothing in the garage other than the chair she's sat in.

'Where I'm sitting,' she says.

'I didn't need a nurse,' I say.

'You need a doctor, but I'll take that as a thank you all the same. I suggest you take a shower. Vince dropped off some of his gear for you to wear.' She shows me a pile of clothes draped over a stool. A black T-shirt and jeans.

Holly gives me some space. I hold my head and ruffle the short crop that is my hair.

My hands are filthy, I stink. Holly can be front of house for a while. I need to get my head together.

* * *

At midday, Vince phones to tell me there'll be an NCA surveillance team out today – not on Nines, on me. He's getting ready to send them out. I'm instructed to carry on as normal. I need to get out.

'Hey, I'm off. I need to prep for tomorrow, charge phones, and all that shit.'

Holly looks up from her work. 'Can I join you? We know Nines is lying low until he calls you. A few people have walked past, so word will be out that we've been here,' she says.

I need to be alone, but figure being with Holly shows willingness to Vince and Winter.

'You can drive,' I tell her.

She kills the garage lights. I cover the Audi, grab my jacket, and we leave. The door self-locks and the alarm sets.

'Have you seen the first foot surveillance?' she asks discreetly.

I have. She's on the opposite side of the street trying to look as though she knows the area. Her mannerisms and casual glances in our direction aren't encouraging. Vince lied about his timing.

'Let's walk towards her,' I say.

Holly hesitates, but I'm already crossing the road, causing a cyclist to swerve to avoid me. He gives me the finger as he looks back.

I need to draw the surveillance out of cover. I need to see as many as I can. Hopefully, this will force the team leader to switch tactics before we get to Holly's car. The garage has enough vehicles in bays now, we had to park our own elsewhere.

The surveillance is trying to avoid eye contact. She walks past and I lightly bump her.

'Sorry, I wasn't looking where I was going,' she says and carries on walking.

I could have been wrong about her.

Holly unlocks her car. I get in the passenger side. I dispense with my seat belt, locking it in place behind me to stop the alarm pinging. If I need to evade the surveillance team, I can exit quickly. They'll be looking for me reaching out for the seat belt as an indication I intend to leave the car.

'I parked in the best spot for the NCA team to plot up. We need to be covered, Sam. I need to feel observed, not out on a limb,' Holly says, engaging the engine.

I can empathise with her concern for safety. The last occasion she was working in my vicinity was not healthy for her in that regard – stuck in a basement club as an enforcer for a major villain. She can hold her own, though. I've witnessed it and seen the skills she employs. People who used the club respected her close-combat skills and would leave when told. We could work well together if she were on the same page as me in terms of results.

Winter is making a statement by bringing her old team back. She wants me, and not in a good way. She's not as in control as she thinks. I intend to abuse her tactics.

The first junction we approach is clear of plain-clothes plod. Holly takes a right. She carries on towards the next main junction and stops for a red light. A queue forms behind her as she keeps the engine running. I check her nearside wing mirror. Three cars back is the Russians' motor I used the other night. A head appears from the rear and leans forward to speak with the driver.

The driver's positioned the car over to the nearside so he can see our Mini.

'We've got company. Three cars back. A black Range Rover. Three subjects as far as I can make out. I know the car from the estate. Which way are you taking?' I say.

Holly looks straight ahead. The lights move from red to amber.

'I see it. Leave it with me. Watch out for any of our lot. Let's hope they've got a visual on us,' she says.

The lights turn to green. We're third in line as the front two cars turn left. Holly indicates left and moves to make the turn. In a last-minute change, she floors it straight. The Range Rover weaves right, looking for the overtake that isn't presenting itself.

'Take the next right,' I say.

Holly palms the wheel and the Mini veers right. A school-crossing warden is in the street with his warning stick up. Children meander across the road. I know what I'd do, but I'm not the one driving. Holly U-turns and heads towards the Range Rover.

She mounts the pavement as the Range Rover moves to block her path. She steadies the car as it travels past the Range Rover and thumps back to the road. The rear snakes before the tyres grip. There's a roundabout ahead. She continues straight.

The Range Rover isn't in sight. Holly slows to an acceptable speed for the residential streets and steadies her breathing.

'We lost them. Great work,' I say.

I see a bus up ahead. As she approaches the back of it, she slows to a stop.

'I'll be in touch.' I open the door and bail out. I've had enough company for one day.

Before Holly can react, I'm on the bus, and away. There's no foot following.

As I stare out of the rear window, I can see a vehicle five cars back from the bus. The driver is looking to move forward. He hasn't seen me; he's concentrating on Holly. I sink into the seat and observe, as the car moves past, the passenger pointing towards the Mini; then my bus turns off and heads east.

34

I'm back at the industrial unit. Vince phoned while I was on the bus. A group meeting's been called. Venue – Ikea car park, Wembley. He sounded calm. Holly had explained what happened and surveillance confirmed that the Range Rover was trying to take us out. The occupants have been identified too: Nines, Sugar, and an unidentified male. The slippery fuck was looking for more than a chat. He could have phoned if he wanted that. I had no idea it was them. They were too far away for me to identify. When we passed them on the footway, I'd ducked.

Nines is becoming volatile. The safest thing for him would be to lie low and let the heat go down. The reassurance patrols will last a week, if that. Crime doesn't stop because of murder, and they'll be needed elsewhere as policing priorities shift.

I sit and detach my leg. My stump is red but not inflamed, which is a good sign. I use the bar area as balance and recharge the battery in the prosthetic. The charge lasts well, but I need to be reassured its energy levels are optimised.

The meeting with Vince is set for later this evening. He's stood Holly and me down. He understands that we need to recharge too. I grab a drink and sit at the bar. Vince will call if he needs us. SO15 are struggling to get a number for Nines, which suits me. Vince has the NCA trying to find the Range Rover and identify the third occupant. Vince is old school. He'll keep the NCA team occupied with other duties until he calls them. After today's jaunt, he won't want the targets spooked despite Commander Barnes' and Winter's wishes. Vince wants this lot taken out his way. I also wonder why the Range Rover was interested in taking us out. My money's on the head of the Russian crew wanting words. It would appear I'm a person of interest to them.

Nines hasn't called. He may have other things on his mind. Something's shifted. There are other agents now imposing their own agendas. Nines will be feeling that he's being ordered about by the Russians.

I grab my leg and use a folded stepladder as a walking aid. I need to shower and change.

I'm certain Nines will call. I need to be ready to respond. Vince's T-shirt and trousers will remain my choice of clothing. To change into anything different could alert Vince that I have another crash pad with clothing. Part of me suspects this was the real reason he would give up his own wardrobe rather than provide cash to buy new threads.

After the shower, I reattach my left limb and get dressed. I'm ready to go. I have everything I need and won't be back for a while. I have the money from the ATM in a bag; I sling it in the Ford.

I park in a side street near Ikea, get out, and walk to the car park. The shop is still open. I see Vince standing by the boot of his car. He's just come out of the store, judging by his full blue bag.

'Good tradecraft, Vince. Glad to see you've not forgotten the basics,' I say.

'Funny. Never shop in your own time when it can be done at work,' he says.

Holly joins us.

'Where's Winter?' I say.

'She's waiting for us in the restaurant. Let's go.' Vince closes his boot and heads inside.

Winter has occupied a table. Everyone's too interested in what they're eating to be bothered with four covert cops having a meeting. We order drinks quickly as Winter needs to be away.

'Glad you could all make it,' she says. 'I'll be brief. Vince can bring you properly up to speed. The Range Rover is known to the Human Trafficking Unit; they've been trying to track it down. Thanks to Vince and my old NCA team, we've saved them a job. Nines and Sugar were in it, caught on a traffic camera. The car is linked to your deceased neighbours, Sam. An obvious embarrassment to me when the Met chose the flat to house you in.' This bit of information I love – it's an acknowledgement of failure or, at the very least, poor judgement.

'I'm not making a complaint,' I say.

Winter doesn't react, just looks at the others, then continues.

'It is believed the girl in hospital was one of many this group have trafficked for sexual exploitation.' Winter pauses and drinks. 'The Trafficking Unit will liaise with the murder team and assist that side of the operation, leaving us with Nines and Sugar. Sam, you've been authorised to drive the targets for this operation. You will not be armed. Phones must be kept on from now until the operation concludes. Vince, call me if you need anything. Good luck.' Winter finishes, takes her cup and places it on a tray trolley.

'Right, drink up,' Vince says. 'Sam, just respond to what Nines asks. Holly, be near a phone. Sam, I'll have you covered both in and out of the Audi. I'll be leading the strike team. You've nothing to worry about.'

'Nothing to worry about? What the fuck, Vince. It's going to be an armed blagging where I'm in the crossfire. How and when do I give you a signal to take them out?' I say.

'Tactics evolve depending on what's happening at the time. You know what you need to know to do your role and that's it. If I thought there was a huge risk to you, then I'd pull you out now. Fact is, I've got the best chance I'll have of taking this lot out once and for all, but I still need you in the mix.'

Vince gets up and Holly does too. One thing's for certain, unless I contact Vince, I'm expected to be doing what I'm told and that's it.

'Do you need a lift?' Holly says to me.

'I'm good. I'll stay at the garage and babysit the Audi. At least from there I can react quickly if Nines calls. I'll let you know when he does though, and I mean that on this occasion.'

Holly agrees.

I give them time to leave. I have another coffee and some food before I head back to the garage and the camp bed. No briefing with a firearms team, so they already know it's me driving. I hope it goes smoothly. I feel this is getting beyond Vince and Winter's capacity to effectively deal with. There are multiple interests, some from bigger players than Nines and Sugar, and they are being underestimated as far as my safety is concerned. Winter seems happy to let Vince take the lead, even if that goes against Commander Barnes' wish to have me on a constant watch until this is over. It looks like it was all lip service on her part to keep the commander happy. She'll have recorded her request.

35

Sunlight breaches the window blinds of the garage kitchen. A ray hits the stainless steel of the kettle, dazzling me awake. I pull the sleeping bag over my face. I don't feel ready to face this day. Memories of my foster father slapping me awake invade my hazy mind. Brutality that refuses to fade away. Violence becomes a way of life, and I'm not immune to its spell. My threshold for physical pain is high. The morphine helps with that. Less so for the emotional pain.

Today is the day of reckoning. Time slows as I wait for noon to turn the phone on. My need for job satisfaction builds. As much as the police want results, so do the criminals. I include myself among them.

It's no longer about the money. It's all about that moment of glory.

I roll back the sleeping bag. There's no turning back. I must get up, face my demons and whatever comes my way. I have the money in the Ford. I must dispose of it but I can't concentrate on that now.

My phone beeps with a text from Holly.

You fit?

I confirm I am.

I get dressed, pull the cover from the Audi, and check it over. It has a full tank of fuel, oil is good, and the engine starts clean. I check the tyre pressure and increase the bars. The modifications make it heavier and I need it to grip the road.

I hear bashing on the garage door. It's too early for any callers. I exit via the fire door and inch my way to the front of the garage. Sugar stands there alone.

'No Nines this morning?'

Sugar startles. 'Fuck. You shit me up with your creeping around.'

'A little early for you?' I say.

Sugar hesitates, then replies, 'Let's go inside. We can talk there.'

I nod and he follows me in via the fire door.

'What's up?' I ask when we're inside. 'We're not meant to meet till later.'

Sugar lifts his padded coat and pulls out a Smith & Wesson Bodyguard .38 Special. It's black with a snub nose and looks used. He tries to hand me the gun, grip first.

'I drive. I don't carry. Just like the last time. Get you in and out.'

Sugar's having none of it. 'This is yours until the job's done,' he says, waving the pistol at me.

I motion towards the worktop, for him to place it there. He's wearing gloves. I'm not. He places it down.

'Why are you giving me this now and not at the meet?'

Sugar looks aghast. 'If you don't turn up with the Audi and strapping that piece then you're a dead man walking. Nines ain't no fool. He's taking shit from the Turks and the Russians. He wants you tooled up.'

'I'll turn my phone on at midday. I'll do what needs doing. As for the piece, you'll get it back when we're done,' I say.

Sugar's shoulders relax. 'Grab your shit,' he says.

This, I hadn't expected. 'That wasn't the plan,' I say.

'Plans change. We're gonna squat somewhere together so we're ready to move as one. Nines wants us with the Audi. Let's go. I'll get the other guns,' Sugar says.

I put on some rubber garage gloves, make sure the safety of the .38 is on and put it in my bag. I place the bag between my legs on the floor of the Audi. It has Velcro on the underside and sticks to the carpet. It won't move as I drive and makes access to the gun easier should I need it. I take one last look at the garage.

'Sugar, press the red button to close the doors once I'm out with the car,' I say.

Sugar nods and does as I say.

The covert camera in the garage will show it's empty and that the last person to see me leave was Sugar. Other than that, I'm on my own.

Sugar has his own run about, a VW Golf GTI, lowered suspension, and profile tyres on polished alloys. He has his ride. I have mine. He's chosen to speed up to create some distance from me and the firearms he's stashed in the adapted half of the Audi's petrol tank. I'm to follow him to our next destination. A round of mirror checks shows nothing unusual in terms of surveillance.

Vince and Winter have a job to do, and so do I. The only person I regret not contacting is Holly. But she knows I was alive this morning, or at least that my phone was on me. Although anyone could have replied on my behalf if they had my phone.

Sugar's driving according to the highway code. He's four cars ahead. I maintain a road position where I can see his vehicle. Every now and then, I notice he's looking in the side mirror. Neither of us acknowledges the other.

The journey's uneventful. I use the time to get composed. Playing both sides has its advantages. I easily become the criminal and not the cop. It was tough to make the transition at first, but eventually street-level drug buys became second nature. Different people, different locations, but still the same outcome. They got nicked and I walked away. The problems came when I saw how much money could be made. I learnt from the ground up. The business end, I learnt from top-level criminals.

Sugar turns into a commercial trading estate in Bull Lane. Small warehousing and trade premises. Some provide sales, others act as storage units. I follow his tail lights to a building that sits neatly at the back of a plot with a large playing field behind it.

Sugar parks up and I roll alongside him. I think of how Vince could manage a surveillance team here. I know he'll struggle, as will Winter's NCA lot. There's one exit in and out. If your face isn't known, attention will be drawn. Sugar comes towards me. There are a few workers shifting crates by forklift. They pay me no attention.

A large door opens to a warehouse and he indicates I need to drive in. I do as he says. As I enter the building there's a distinct smell of fish. Inside is cool. Thick Styrofoam cases stand tall around the walls along with industrial refrigerators and freezers. A man in a white lab coat and mask shows me where he wants the Audi. I ease the bag off the carpet of the driver's floor, sling the strap over my shoulder and get out. The man in the coat requests the keys.

'If you need it moving, just ask,' I say.

He's still holding out his hand wagging his fingers like Neo from *The Matrix*.

Nines appears from behind some long strips of plastic that separate the room from a side area.

'Give him the keys,' he says.

My heart beats faster. There's an insistence on control of the car that can only mean they wish to sweep it for tracking devices or add something to it that I'm not to know about.

I reluctantly pass the key fob over. Nines joins me and puts his arm around my shoulder.

'I'll give you a tour of the factory,' he says. 'See what you make of my young business mind.'

We make our way towards some floor-to-ceiling plastic separators. Nines goes through first and bats the sheets away. Sugar and I follow. Sugar isn't taking in the building, which means he's seen all this before.

I soak up as much information as I can: exit points, windows, any overt weapons. Aside from fish knives on boxes and benches where workers gut carcasses, there's nothing obvious. Ahead of us is what appears to be a vault door. Nines places his thumb on a pad and the door unlocks. He needs two hands to pull it open and he waves us into a lab and money exchange. No one looks up. Cash is being bagged up in thousand-pound bundles. Cocaine is being mixed and prepped with another white powder of similar consistency.

'What's the mix?' I say, curiosity getting the better of me.

'It's a blend of coke, ketamine, and talcum powder. Enough to floor a horse, shower it, then pamper the fucker after,' Nines proudly announces.

He gestures to a worker who cuts a line from a mound of powder.

'Give it a try, but I warn you, this shit kicks like a mule. You won't suffer, that block is pure,' Nines says.

'I need to be fit for tonight,' I say.

Nines rolls his eyes and does the line himself. He points to the guy behind the desk, who cuts another wedge, wraps it, bags it, and gives it him.

'A gift for when we're done,' he says, handing me the bag.

I pocket it.

Nines is holding it together, so I figure it's a good mix. His eyes start showing signs of the drug's movement through his body as he relaxes and licks his gums and upper lip.

A fish crate is brought into the room. I watch as bundles of notes are stacked in a false compartment sealed in waterproof bags and more ice is put over them. Another false floor is added, and more fish and ice thrown inside to finish off the appearance. Once the lid is on, the crate leaves. Where to? I don't know.

'What's with the extra ice over the cash?' I say.

Nines eyes me in his semi-stoned state. A state I'm trying to take advantage of.

'Each crate gets put on a lorry for distribution. If the lorry is stopped then it's expected to weigh what it should if it was stacked up with fish. We add some thin lead strips in the bundles, so everything appears good. So far, we ain't had any bother. Stick with me, man. You'll learn so much you could be running this end of the line. Rather than getting engine oil all over you, you'd be covered in powder and money. Let's go.'

Nines sets off through another door. We enter a rest area for the workers. I thought my conditions in the garage were bad, but this takes the piss. No wonder no one's raided it. The workers don't leave here unless they're dead. That thought I shove to one side and pat the bag for comfort. I hope the .38 is match fit.

* * *

Winter is pondering how she could extract herself from a laborious finance meeting when her phone flashes with Vince's name on the screen.

'I need to take this,' she says, leaving the room and stepping into the foyer outside.

'Winter here.'

'We've got a situation. I know you hate surprises, and this is one I could have done without too.'

'Go on,' Winter says.

'I had the foresight to put a covert surveillance officer on the garage and half of my team on standby. I'm glad I trusted my gut especially when they reported Sugar arriving, early doors. The guns were removed from the box and into the concealed space in the Audi. Sam was alone. It was impossible for him to make contact. From what was fed back to me, I think Sam was taken on the hop. By the way, the surveillance officer described him surprising Sugar outside the garage. Holly is at the garage while this develops. I need her there in case they return.'

'What else?' Winter says, sensing she hadn't been told everything.

'There's a major issue. The garage camera shows Sugar giving Sam a .38 special handgun. No bullets were seen. I'm treating the weapon as live. Their conversation was recorded. Sam makes it clear to Sugar that he doesn't carry guns. He wasn't given any choice. Not to have accepted the gun could have compromised his safety.' Vince pauses while Winter takes in the information.

'Okay. We can only deal with what we know at this point in the operation. Is there anything else?'

Vince sighed. 'I got the other half of my team deployed as soon as I got the call from my officer. They were waiting nearby. They followed and are now in the vicinity of an industrial site in N18. Sugar and Sam have been seen but there's no visual now. They're in a food preparation premises. Initial research shows it as belonging to Fresh 2 Fry – a fish preparation and storage company.

'The environment is poor for surveillance. A loose containment is the best I can achieve at present. Intelligence is being developed and liaison with our SO15 colleagues is proving useful; they have other intelligence feeds from phone chatter they're picking up from a line they have on the Russians. The name Nines has been heard in conversation and it's believed he is there too.'

'Great work. Keep me updated as this develops,' Winter says.

36

A set of metal stairs leads to an upper floor and open-plan space. A man is sat in a leather chair smoking a pencil-size cigar. He turns in my direction.

'Drink?' he says, with a Russian lilt to his voice.

'Whatever you're having,' I say.

Nines and Sugar sit as the Russian goes to a desk drawer and pulls out a bottle of vodka.

He's late twenties, casually dressed, shaved head, and no visible tattoos. He has the air of a businessman who gets what he wants. He hands me a drink and sits in a chair opposite me.

'Your woman at the garage is a good driver, a very skilled driver.'

His emphasis on the word skilled isn't lost on me. 'She can handle herself if that's what you mean,' I say.

He stands and looks at an old print of a street in a London borough.

'Your country has history, just like mine. I know my history, but yours is unclear. I'm interested in your history and that of your boss. These two gentlemen have told me a lot about you both. Your business, your background in the military, and your ability to arrange adapted transport at short notice.' He turns to face me and leans on the table, glass in hand.

Nines and Sugar say nothing.

'In the spirit of openness, I have let you see my business and how I operate. I want to know more about how your enterprise works. How does a garage make money when it's closed most of the time with the same cars on the ramps? Strange, don't you think?'

This isn't going how I expected. Nines has drawn me into a trap.

They have me where they want me. Either the Russian will work with me or decide I'm not good for trade and kill me, then have Nines and Sugar dispose of the body. They've already planted the .38 special on me. Why else would he show me his business?

I'm hoping he sees sense in using me to work with him. I need to play strong. Weakness will be pounced upon.

'What I do is my business and what you do is yours. Mine won't affect yours and vice versa. There's space for us both to move where we need to, I can assure you of that.'

'I'm afraid that won't do, Mr Sky. You see, I don't like people who foul my footway and expect me to clean it up. Like a stray dog, you have found your way to my family, begging to eat food from my table. Your boss demonstrated very good driving skills when she outran my car. Why would she take such dangerous tactics when she could have pulled over and seen it was Nines and Sugar? People she knows. People you know.'

His eyes never leave mine. He's evaluating everything, verbal and non-verbal. He's shrewd, very shrewd.

'That, I can answer. I saw on the news what happened at my flat. It got taken over by people I don't know. Next thing, the same Range Rover I'd seen being 'guarded' on my estate is wanting to catch up with me. I panicked and told Kat to lose you. She's not a princess, she knows the score, Mr…?'

'My name is not your business, but your explanation is reasonable. I'm told you also drive well and know how to handle yourself. I can use that too. I would've told you the same had you stopped the other day. I was in the car.' He pauses, watching my reaction, then resumes. 'You will handle all repairs to my fleet, both at your premises, and away, should I call on you. If you refuse, you and your boss will be history. Don't refuse or give false promises in the hope I'll go away, Mr Sky. That would be the worse decision you could make. Tonight's work you will do as an act of goodwill. If all goes well, you will be rewarded appropriately beyond the bag of powder you were given downstairs and the pistol you're carrying. I'll arrange new accommodation for you now the police have taken over your flat.'

He sounds determined not to give me any options.

The Russian leans back in his chair. 'Why am I making this pact? Nines and Sugar say you're useful. You have evaded police and can handle yourself in stressful situations. I admire this. I'm a few men down. I need to replace them with someone who doesn't stand out and can do the job of three men. When you get back to your car, load the gun with the bullets that will be in your side door before you leave. The streets are dangerous.'

He stops, and Nines stands; a clear indication that the introduction is over. Whatever I said corroborated what Nines had told him and what the dead Russians would have reported back when they were alive. I've been so embroiled in the deception of my own force that I underestimated the capability of the other side to carry out their own surveillance. Lesson learnt. I'd got off lightly and by the relieved look on Nines' face, he realises that too. He's sobered up now. I still have my bag of white.

I'm glad the gun's not loaded. What concerns me is what the Russian with no name wants from me. Nines has been tight-lipped about tonight's show. I can understand why. He's no big shot.

Nines and Sugar don't speak as we leave the environs of the Russian oligarch. The elegance of the open-plan area makes way to the squalor of a break room with a vending machine stocked with multi-buy packets of crisps and soft drinks. Nines presses a couple of buttons and the machine whirs into life and drops a can of fake coke and foreign crisps.

'They're free, help yourself; we've got a long wait.' Nines sits down and pulls the ring off his can. The drink fizzes over as he leans forward, shaking his hands and cursing.

I take a spare plastic chair. My nose has now adjusted to the stench of fish and contraband. A British bulldog wanders in, swaggers over to Nines, and starts licking up the overspill from between his feet. Nines kicks out as the mutt takes a fancy to his leg.

'Fuckin' dog, shouldn't even be on a premises that preps food, for fuck's sake.'

The dog comes where I'm sat and lies down. I've never had much time for animals, especially dogs. Too needy for my liking.

'So, which one of you is buying lunch?' I ask.

Sugar and Nines don't look impressed.

'No one is eating nothing unless it's crisps. We stay here until we move out,' Sugar says.

'I need to be alert for the drive and that won't happen by eating out-of-date crisps. I don't give a fuck what your man upstairs says. I'm going out to eat. I'll bring something back for you two.'

I move to get up. Nines demands that I stay. I judge he's serious by the .38 Special he's produced from behind his back. The dog looks up from beside me and I sit back down.

'I see your Russian got a job lot of Specials. What about you, Sugar? You packing?' I say.

Sugar doesn't reply.

I smirk. 'I hope yours has bullets, Nines. If it doesn't, I'm going on a lunch run.'

Nines isn't happy at the challenge.

'Of course it's loaded, you prick! We ain't gonna give you a loaded gun until we're on the road and well on top of the game. Whatever he says, you'll get the bullets when I fucking decide you need them,' he says.

I pat the dog. It rolls over for a belly rub.

'You don't like being bossed about, do you, Nines?' I continue. 'I bet the Russian has you running around his empire all day and night. You're too inexperienced for this game. Stick to nicking phones, far easier for you.'

Nines is straight over, gun at my forehead. The bulldog's out the door.

'Shut the fuck up,' Nines bellows.

I put my hands in the air.

Nines steps between my legs, the gun barrel disappears in my peripheral vision. I smash my left arm down on his wrist, knocking the gun off target. I spring up, head-butting the bridge of his nose.

He drops the gun. Sugar reacts. I bring my left leg up and into Nines' groin. He falls back into Sugar. I pull my right leg towards me and kick my foot forward, sole out flat. It connects with Sugar. He goes to the ground along with Nines. I pick up the .38 Special and check the weapon. It's empty. I throw the gun at Nines.

'All you had to do was say. It would've saved you a lot of tears. When do we get the ammo? Or do we?'

Nines has crawled back to his seat and leans forward, clutching at his stomach muscles, willing the pain to stop. I give him time to recover his breath to speak, but Sugar takes over.

'Tell him, man. Tell him what shit's going down. We're all in it, for fuck's sake, and he might have a better idea than you about surviving it,' Sugar says.

Nines shakes his head in disgust at his mate's lack of loyalty. I wait for the truth to out. If it doesn't, I plan to beat the living shit out of them both until I know what I'm in for. This isn't any old cash-in-transit robbery we're involved in. No Russian with the connections, wealth, and power the man upstairs has would be associating with this scum unless no one else was stupid enough to get involved.

No wonder the man upstairs wasn't pressing in his questioning. He doesn't expect us to survive the trip. Hence the tour of his empire. All smoke and mirrors. He doesn't expect us to live to see it again.

'He ain't giving us any bullets until we're in the Audi. That's why the car ain't with us right now. It's elsewhere getting loaded up. Look, if I'd have told you it ain't no box run we were on, then you could have left us. I needed a driver who would take no shit. You're it. You showed me that the other night in Muswell Hill. You do this run for me, you'll get left alone to work with him upstairs as much as you want. He's got London covered for girls and coke. He's in with some heavy players who let him work their areas for a cut. He ain't stupid. He needs protection,' Nines says, exasperated.

'What's the deal tonight?' I say, calmly.

Nines is pacing the room, the gun left on his chair.

'I can't tell you right off. If I do, he'll sniff a rat, and I ain't no grass. All you've got to do is drive. Trust me, you won't be needing no piece or nothing for this work. Me and Sugar are the boys on the ground. You just need to be ready to get us away as soon as we get back in the motor.'

'Why give me a gun with no ammo, hours before a job where I won't need one? You're not very good at this game, are you?' I say.

Nines stops pacing.

'Let me tell you summat. I fucking ran that estate like no other before this firm took over. I had it tight between me, Toots, and Sugar. The Russians recruited Toots. Tried to have me taken out by some street punk kid when I wouldn't play ball. I ain't into abusing girls for cash. It's strictly drugs with me. But this guy ain't going away. I had to come on board with him. I told him you was in the market for a gun. Told him you'd do it for that and a cash bonus of a grand.'

Nines shifts the gun between his hands in a state of anxious tension. He knows he hasn't got the army to take out the Russians and he thinks the Turks do, hence the killings. He either goes underground or works with the head man to stay protected. The problem is he is now in the Russian's pocket. A pocket that has unknown depths. Nines either plays the game or dies. Those are his options.

'What other scams have you got going that the Russian guy doesn't know about?' I say, more for my own knowledge.

'What d'you mean?' Nines asks.

'You know what I mean. I'm not just a "mechanic", you realise that from what you've seen. I dabble in other things too. You must have an ace up your sleeve. A part of your business that belongs just to you,' I say.

Nines smiles, as does Sugar.

'We got a small racket going. A group of wannabe dealers who go out and rob for us. Nothing big, just phones and shit. It's a steady little earner though. Last week they came back from Holborn with a nice string of medals from a tramp and a wedge of cash from some rich bitch. Medals must be worth summat the way he fought for them. He got what he deserved though,' Nines says.

The answer takes me by surprise. 'What do you mean, how he fought for them?' I say.

'He put up a mean fight. One of my fella's videoed it to show me how well they did. He's in hospital. At least he's got bed, food, and clean clothes. They done him a favour.'

Nines and Sugar laugh.

I focus on my role, but the well of anger within me is boiling. These two boys really are the lowest of the low.

'Where are the medals now?' I say.

'Why? You interested in them?' Sugar says.

'I know a guy who might be in the market for them.'

'One thing at a time. Get this shit sorted tonight then we can talk about the medals and coming on board with that side of the business too,' Nines says, checking his watch. 'You got the phone I gave you?'

I look at my bag near a chair by the floor.

'Switch it on,' Nines says, as he and Sugar turn theirs on.

I get up, and take out the phone along with the handgun. I switch it on, and it pings to life. Then, I put the phone and the gun on the table. 'I've got no signal,' I say.

'You won't get one until we're out of here. You'll get a text with a postcode on it. You put the code in the car's sat nav, follow it until we get there, then wait. That's it. When we get back in the car, we head back here. Make sure you know the route in reverse. No code in the system on the return leg,' Nines says.

I agree. Asking questions would be useless. Whatever's going to happen, I must react as I go. I hope Vince and his team are all over this. For once, I'm nervous about the outcome.

I spend the rest of the wait cleaning the gun. I have no rags, but Sugar hands me a bandana from his pocket. They watch as I work and neither asks questions. Nines passes me his gun to clean, too. It bides the time. It all reminds me of downtime before a live police operation. Our operational feeding on this occasion isn't up to the police standards, but waiting for the word to "go" is the same. The main difference is the firearms here are illegal with no bullets, and my team is my enemy. Enemies inside and out surround me.

One consolation is that neither Nines nor Sugar suspect I'm undercover Old Bill. I enjoy handling the .38 Special. I've fired one before on weapons familiarisation courses in the army and police. It's not the killing power that I like. It's the mundane cleaning of it that stills my mind and keeps me focused. Nines and Sugar are slowly losing their shit, both pacing to and from the vending machine, stopping occasionally to dispense crisps and drink.

The gun's new. If there's ammunition in the car, then I'm loading it, authorised or not. If questioned, I'll put it all down to keeping in role or failing that, plain old duress. Duress sounds better.

Nines throws me some crisps and a coke.

'Eat and drink. There's not much longer to go now.'

I catch what's thrown and put the weapon down. Nines takes back his gun. I place mine back in my bag. As I do, a phone is heard ringing. It's Nines' phone he's just turned on. He must be on a different network to me.

He says nothing, just listens, grunts then says, 'Sweet.' He puts the phone in his pocket.

'Car's ready. Let's go.'

37

Nines and Sugar hunker down in the back seat. Night has fallen. Between them they have a Skorpion automatic pistol, a loaded .38 Special and an Anonymous mask each. I don't have the privilege of matching headwear. I'm given a balaclava. There can only be one reason why. I'm a target who, for recognition purposes, will be the one wearing a balaclava. After all, I'm just the driver. I still have no ammo.

The Audi was handed back with no questions asked. I feel uncomfortable. From the mood of the two in the back, this doesn't feel good. They both look resigned to conducting the will of the foreign power that sits on his mighty throne.

The Russian is no longer at the premises. He left when the valet handed back the keys to the Audi. There were no goodbyes, just a nod at me as he entered the Range Rover that Nines had been using. I know I won't be seeing the Russian again, call it a sixth sense.

I adjust the internal mirror and mess about with the seat adjustments, much to the annoyance of the two in the back.

I need to see if anything is strapped under the driver's seat, like an IED. I'm relieved. It all feels as it should be. My tracker is still in place – not a lot of use now. We move out behind the Range Rover. Another car that's been parked in the unit's yard appears. It's another Range Rover, but dark green. It has privacy glass too.

Anyone would think this is a police close protection run. But there's no intention to protect here. This is a convoy intent on destruction. A war against a rival firm whose territory is about to get a state visit.

Our escort will be looking to act as a decoy car to deter police. I feel the sweat on my brow and wipe it away. The sweat down my back I can do nothing about. I'm going in blind and hope Winter and Vince have eyes on us, or a plan to intercept.

Winter was cautious in her briefing. I surmise she wants the element of surprise to be just that. It's a good thing not knowing if Vince or Winter's old team are out. If I'm overtly looking for the hard-stop, then I'm game on for the two in the back to kill on sight.

'Keep on him,' Nines says.

'I have the sat nav primed like you said. Do I follow that or him in front?' I ask.

'Stick with what I fucking told you,' Nines says.

This means nothing to me so I decide to stick with the sat nav route.

We're in Aldermans Hill. Nines' phone beeps with an incoming message. I see his head dip to look at his screen. The lead Range Rover breaks right into Old Park Road but the sat nav indicates straight on.

'What do you want me to do?' I say as the turning approaches.

'Keep going until I tell you to stop,' Nines says.

I continue straight. The rear vehicle turns right leaving us to run.

We're on the outskirts of Brookmans Park. I check my mirrors and pull over.

'What in the fuck are you doing?' Sugar says.

'I'm letting traffic past.'

'This ain't a time to be a knight of the fucking road!' Sugar says.

I turn and face him. 'Listen up, shit for brains. I'm doing my job and getting you to yours. The sat nav says I'm on top of where you need to be, so leave me to work. You just sit there stroking your toy.' I'm beginning to tire of the weary back seat drivers.

'You what? I should just waste you now, you mouthy fuck!' Sugar barks back.

I move into the traffic again. I don't need any surveillance getting cocky and close.

'So, that's the plan? Waste me once I'm no use? Hardly a fair fight when I've no bullets.' I keep our speed steady.

'Sugar, shut up. Let him do his job,' Nines says.

Sugar slumps back.

There's a nice build-up of cars that will afford any surveillance team good cover if they're out. Vince's lot are good. Winter's lot must have improved, as I'm unaware of any obvious follow. The sat nav screen indicates the time left to our destination is two minutes.

* * *

From Control, all units remain in position and await the next transmission.

Alpha One, from Control, sit rep please.

From Alpha One, targets are out of visual and into commercial premises.

Control from Alpha Three, I have exit and entrance covered in case of movement, over.

All units from Control, maintain positions. Only use radio if active until further notice.

Control out.

A hush descends upon the airwaves. Operators remain busy updating screens and evaluating possible routes away from the area. Winter monitors the outside drone feed.

She stops tapping her pen against the edge of her cheek and rocks from side to side in her swivel chair. A civilian intelligence officer passes her an information log to sign. She scans it and passes it back.

For a moment, she considers Batford, with feelings of concern. She puts the pen down, ties up her hair, and walks over to the main controller.

'Any word from Vince? Has he heard from DS Batford?' she asks.

'Not that I've been made aware of, ma'am. He'll be fine though, he's a resilient one that DS. He'll know what to do, I'm sure he's okay.'

Winter agrees. 'Let me know if our teams see him.'

She returns to her desk and awaits further transmissions. Time passes. Surveillance operatives confirm there are no changes.

Then the radio bursts to life.

Control, from Alpha Three.

Alpha Three, from Control, go ahead.

From Alpha Three, targets are on the move heading west. Two others from the premises, travelling in convoy, flanking target vehicle.

Alpha Three acknowledged by Control. All units, targets are on the move west. I repeat on the move west. Alpha Three, maintain commentary, and pass details of further vehicles involved, Control over.

From Alpha Three, all received.

38

'Fuck it! He's early,' Nines says.

A security van is pulled up in a gravelled parking area opposite what looks like a Turkish social club. I've had no instructions to stop.

Up ahead is a block of flats.

'In here, in here!' Nines says.

'Are you sure? There'll be people everywhere. It's a load of flats, for fuck's sake,' I say.

Nines is having none of it. 'Turn in and keep going right,' he says.

I have no choice. I turn and enter the parking area for the residential building. Most lights are on in the flats, the curtains drawn. No one's outside. Up ahead, there's a single headlight. Either a car with one light out or a motorcycle. As I draw close, the beam becomes brighter, then moves towards me.

'Is this part of the plan? Tell me now,' I say.

Nines ducks down, leaning into the side of the passenger door. That's all I need to know.

I whack our lights on full as the single bright orb approaches, then disappears like a UFO. A single red tail light is all I see. One motorcycle rider dressed all in black, engine over 750cc. I pray it's one of Vince's team.

'Over there, next to that blue van. Park it up nose out,' Nines demands.

The van is a short wheelbase Mercedes, the kind used by local delivery drivers. I park as instructed and turn off the engine. As our lights fade, those from the flats cast a shadow across a patch of grass.

I take the time to remain present, concentrating on each breath, in and out, while considering my options.

'We ain't got much longer to wait, so here it is.' Nines leans forward between the front seats. 'The club we passed with the van outside is getting loaded up with takings, big takings. That van ain't gonna make it. The Turkish fellas at the pool hall – it's their den.

'The Russian got wind of how much they was making cleaning cash from our robberies and other activities. The Russian wants them dead, and he wants that cash too. It's a message of retribution for the killing of his men in your flat. He says they're responsible. The Turks insist on using a legitimate firm to move the money. They have an arrangement with an Arabic bank, that's all I know.'

This isn't good. This lot are looking to commit murder and they won't want any witnesses. It's all crystal clear now. I'll be another body along with whoever is inside. A fired .38 Special placed in my hands. No Russian Skorpion guns used. But they're not thinking this through. There'll be no gun residue on my skin, and they don't know I'm a cop.

For once, I see no way out of this. It's kill or be killed, and they're the ones with the firepower.

'Where do you want me?' I say, hoping they dispel my fears and tell me to stay in the car.

'We need you to load the cash in the Audi while we take care of things inside. We won't have long. There'll be a shit ton of noise,' Nines says. Then he pulls on an Anonymous mask, and Sugar does too.

'Go before we miss the van,' Nines says.

I pull down my balaclava and drive towards the social club. I hit the street and waste no time pulling alongside the van. Nines and Sugar exit the Audi and move towards the door, guns drawn. I get out and wait.

The rear doors to the security van fling open. Cops pile out the back shouting, "Armed police". Armed officers appear from the roof of the club.

A small red dot illuminates my chest.

My heart pounds. I can taste my own spit on the wool of the balaclava. I leave my hands in the air. Nines and Sugar are on the floor at the feet of the armed officers. The area's awash with blue lights from covert and overt cars as more police appear on the scene.

A police helicopter joins the gathering and lights me up from above. A voice from a loud hailer demands I remain where I am with my hands where they can see them.

I glance down at my chest. The one red dot has become a quivering mass of many. I listen intently to the instructions of the armed officer who takes control of my detention.

A German shepherd is straining at the leash, teeth on full display as it barks. Strangely, I feel relieved I'm alive. My job is done. I'm soon on the floor in handcuffs, being searched.

Gradually things calm down and the scene is secured. I'm lifted off the floor, my head forced down to disorientate me. I see the bottom of a car door open. I'm pushed into the rear seats and the door closes. I'm not alone. I recognise the unmistakable sign of Vince's brogues.

Vince moves me forward and cuts the plastic cuffs as our car races away from the scene.

'Let's get you home, eh?' He hands me a bottle of beer.

'Thank fuck you were there, Vince. I think they were going to kill me. There's an unloaded .38 Special on the driver's floor of the Audi and a huge amount of cash in my bag. Nines told me to look after it. Both will have my DNA all over it,' I say.

'Relax, Sam. You're safe. We'll deal with it,' Vince says.

My head flops back against the seat. Now comes the battle with the aftermath of the operation. A dissociated feeling crowds my addled mind as the adrenaline subsides. I try to believe what Vince told me – that I'm safe – but the pounding in my chest tells me that's not true.

* * *

Back at Hendon, I splash my face and neck with cold water. On the journey, Vince explained that the Russian at the industrial site had been on the SO15 watch list and his phone monitored.

They had heard him talk of the plan for the Turkish club. Vince was ahead of the game. The Russian's warehouse was raided, drug factory discovered, money and property seized.

It's all a game in the end. On this occasion, Winter and Vince came out winners.

I step out of the toilet block and back to the office where Vince is getting off the phone to Winter.

'Do you need a lift anywhere?' he asks.

'I'll get a cab. I'll be back tomorrow morning for the mop-up and proper debrief, that's if you don't mind, guv?'

Vince laughs and waves me off. I head out of the gates and find a cab. 'Holiday Inn, Scratchwood, mate.'

The driver sets off.

I make a conscious decision to stay away from any of my new dwellings. I feel too raw to return now the operation is over. I'm glad I told Vince about the .38 Special.

My phone goes, it's Vince.

> Go to Edmonton nick and retrieve Audi
> tomorrow morning. VG.

I read through the message again and reply, "OK". Tonight, I've had enough. I press the key card into the lock of the hotel and the green bar lights up as I enter. The bed welcomes me as I strip down, remove my leg, and collapse.

39

The next morning, at Edmonton, the station officer hands me the Audi key. A driver had brought the vehicle in last night and stored it in the back yard. I throw my bag in the passenger seat and shut the driver's door. I look in the back. There are still signs of the food wrappers and cans Nines and Sugar had brought along for the ride. Vince considered forensically examining the interior but didn't bother. He has all the evidence he needs from his team's surveillance placing the two of them in the car. I too can confirm that. The .38 Special must have been seized, with my bag.

I head towards Hendon for the meeting with Vince and the operational team.

Interviews are taking place this morning. Cordons remain at the food factory unit on the industrial estate, and various other premises linked to the Russian. Nines and Sugar had their flats turned over. A significant haul of stolen property was found there, along with drugs and cash. Vince will tell me if any medals turn up.

I adjust the volume on the Audi's stereo. The speaker begins to crackle intermittently. The last thing I need is to be stuck in traffic with no sounds. I use the technical knowledge I gained from the mechanics course Winter sponsored, and smash the speaker on the door panel with my fist.

The speaker caves in slightly. I pull into a garage and kill the engine. As I open the driver's door, I notice an unmistakable line of white powder. I shut the door, check my mirrors, and move to a side street opposite. I ease the speaker back in place.

Vince hasn't had the Audi searched. The car's packed with cocaine. I now realise why the car was taken away at the Russian's unit. I need to head to my industrial factory, and fast.

Vince doesn't know that the car wasn't with me the whole time. It should be me who informs the lead investigator of anything that took place out of sight and hearing of the surveillance team. It's my role after all. On this occasion, I've been remiss.

* * *

Back at my industrial unit, I gently remove the speaker. The door panel is packed with kilo slabs of cocaine. I remove the speaker on the passenger side and find more. It's a cursory look, but enough to let me know there was more to the job than I thought. The Audi was meant to end up with someone else. Nines? I don't know. Unless the Russian is questioned about the Audi, it won't come up. CCTV from his warehouse may show it being there though. It's a risk.

Little Chris isn't asking for it back yet and Vince wanted it away from the police station yard.

Fuck. I wasn't expecting this. I should do the right thing and call Vince. I look up at Mike's ashes. I know what he'd do. Open a bottle of champagne and toast to success. I sit down with a whisky. What if Vince knows and is setting me up? He can't, though. He'd have had the car lifted at the scene, stripped down, properly forensically examined, and photographed. In all the buzz of the takedown, he's missed a huge trick. But the bottom line is, this one came too close for comfort, and I needed a security option. Thirty thousand pounds seemed like a good personal investment on this occasion.

My mind's spinning. I'd accepted that on this outing I'd lucked out being alive.

I thought with Mike gone it would be easy to stop. The money didn't feel like robbery; it was drug dealer's cash. But this amount of cocaine is huge. Questions will be asked as to where it is. This belongs to a large organised criminal network. They've lost major business in drugs, prostitution, and trafficking thanks to me. If my lot don't ask questions of Nines or the Russian, then the Russian will suspect it's been robbed. Whoever's in charge will stop at nothing to establish by whom.

The police have many leaks aside from me. Cash gets people talking. The sequence of events following the arrests will be worked out and those left standing judged against each other.

It won't take them long to establish who was Old Bill, and come up with me.

Why would they suspect me?

Because I won't be appearing in court. In the worst-case scenario, I'll be giving evidence behind a screen. The investigation is tight. Nines and Sugar will enter a guilty plea to get a reduced sentence. The Russians could suspect Holly, but she will have known too little by the time I was whisked away by Sugar.

I'm sitting on half-a-million-pounds worth of cocaine and the street value is considerably more. I look around me at where I've ended up. All this isn't me. It's Mike. The cars, the premises, the organisation, and the forward planning are all Mike.

I don't do forward planning to Mike's extent. My forward planning consists of how I can get out of what I'm in and survive. With this lot, I could survive very well, very well indeed. I'm no big-time drug supplier though, that was Mike's domain too. He had the contacts and the gift of the gab. I was the supplier; he was the seller. I have some contacts that I only regard as acquaintances.

I change gloves and load the cocaine in a storage cabinet. I need to get the Audi back.

I access the memory card from the car camera and replace it with a different one. When it's examined, there'll will be no data that can be recovered. Hopefully they'll conclude that the technical issues with the system need reviewing and leave it at that. Bad guys are caught. Everyone's happy. Move on.

Sensitive log closing entry

A superb conclusion and an outstanding team effort. What started out as an investigation into a gang involved in armed robbery evolved into a multi-agency disruption of a large organised criminal network involved in international crime.

Commander Barnes has briefed the commissioner, and she is elated at the outcome, as am I. DI Gladwell is satisfied that all avenues have been explored and the investigation can now be closed. The threat against Olivia Koleci has been downgraded and she is being referred to a trafficking charity for further help.

All firearms recovered during the operation have been submitted to the laboratory for forensic work. For the record, a decision was taken to leave the guns in place while the operation ran. The live ammunition was replaced with blank firing rounds and the container the guns were in was subject to monitoring by installed covert cameras.

That said, there was always a chance new ammunition may have been obtained or the targets might have realised that the swap had taken place. Thankfully, despite the risks, this tactic paid off and no one was injured or killed.

DS Batford was NOT made aware of this. It was decided that it was in his best interest and safety not to know so that he would act naturally and not raise the targets' suspicions.

DI Gladwell was accurate in his planning and assessment. I look forward to working with him again in the future.

Finally, Mike Hall's widow, Yvonne Hall, has met with the source handlers from Professional Standards following her initial chat with me, regarding DS Batford. The handler has said it's a relationship that will be very worthwhile.

DI Gladwell has insisted on writing commendations for both DC Holly Burns and DS Sam Batford for professionalism and detective ability.

There's little I can do about the commendation for DS Batford. On this occasion, he would appear to have acted in the best interest of the inquiry, something I never thought I would write in an official log.

Case closed.

Klara Winter – Detective Superintendent
Covert policing
Authorising officer
Op Envy

40

Two weeks have passed since the operation ended. All targets remanded in custody are awaiting sentencing after entering early pleas of guilty.

This is a welcome relief to us all. Especially me. I've had time to reflect on all that happened. I miss Holly. I never thought I'd find myself thinking that, but on this outing, she was good to work with and comfortable to have around.

I'm back at the park where I met the old soldier. I've been back several times but haven't been able to find him. As I walk towards the museum, thinking this is another wasted journey, I see what looks like a pile of dumped clothes on the ground. I then see the mound move and the outline of a pair of boots. If it isn't him, it could be someone who knows him.

I approach and the person turns. It's the soldier. His hair is neater than when I first met him. His beard is short. The hospital must have cleaned him up. He looks at me warily, no hint of recognition that would suggest he remembers me. I show him my warrant card.

'Are you Richard Donaldson formally of the Royal Scots?' I ask.

He leans in and looks closely at the card. It's mine, under my true identity.

'Yes. What have I done wrong?' he says, gathering his carrier bags around him like he's building a fort.

'Nothing. I'm not here to move you on.' I sit down beside him. 'You were the victim of a robbery,' I say.

'Yes. I was. The bastards got away with my medals and what little cash I had. Five pounds and forty-three pence, if I'm not mistaken. Have you come for a further statement? I can't add anything more. I told the officer all I could remember and that wasn't much.' He scratches at his beard.

'I've come to see if you recognise these.'

From my pocket, I take the exhibits bag containing the medals found at Nines' flat. I know they're his. The army confirmed the service number engraved on them and gave me his details. He looks at the bag and back at me as he reaches out and takes them, turning them over in his soiled hands.

'These are my medals, but they weren't like this when they took them.'

'I hope you don't mind. I took the liberty of having them cleaned and mounted for you,' I say.

Teary eyes stare back at me. I take the medals and motion for him to lean forwards, which he does. I pin the even line of medals to his jumper. He looks down and smiles as he fastens his jacket over them.

'I need you to sign this statement saying they've been returned,' I explain. 'The gang who took them have all been nicked. They're serving time for your robbery and other offences.'

I shake his hand and get up. As I start to leave, he speaks. 'You're a good man, DS Batford. Look after yourself and thank you.'

41

I watch Yvonne Hall as she leaves the salon. It's not the first time I've watched her. Since the operation finished, I've had time to assess how her life is going. A good DS is always mindful of people's welfare. That includes the welfare of an ex-detective's widow.

She's smartly dressed in black leather trousers and a white blouse. She does a final check on the door then pulls down a grill for extra measure. She appears relaxed and happier than when we last met. She looks about before getting in her car then heads off. I'd contacted her using a burner phone, saying I needed to meet before I disposed of Mike's ashes.

I told her it had been too painful to do it sooner, and work had prevented me. She'd agreed to meet at a neutral venue I chose, away from prying eyes. She's been doing her best to get on with her life since the funeral. She's also met some new friends, which hasn't gone unnoticed.

We meet at a tea hut on the edge of Epping Forest. It will be closed now, it's 9 p.m. She had a late client; it was best to see her once she was done. From what I observed, there was more than one client. And the fact that one was bald hadn't escaped my notice. The female wore a hat. It wasn't her first visit, and I wonder what treatment required such frequency.

I needed to ensure Yvonne would be alone when she left work so I follow in my car at a distance. The roads get darker as she skirts around the edge of the forest in her Fiat 500. She finds the tea hut and parks up.

The area's empty of cars and set back from the road in a secluded clearing. My Tesla quietly crawls along. The internal monitor screen is on night mode. I stop, park, and get out of the car. I can see her from where I am. She's parked nose in, which is ideal.

I move away from the Tesla and open the car's app on my phone. I press on the headlights function. The car's lights flash on and off as I sit back in the woods.

She's seen the agreed sign. Her door opens and the interior light shines then dims as she shuts the door. She walks tentatively towards the Tesla, phone to her ear. I feel my phone vibrate, then stop. She reaches the car, looking about as she approaches, using the light from her phone to see. As she gets closer, I activate the passenger door opening function. She startles as it opens, looks about, then checks inside the car. On the driver's seat is a plain box with a yellow Post-it attached. On it is written "IOU". She picks it up and looks around.

Her phone screen lights up her face. She appears relaxed as she takes the parcel back towards her car.

She opens her car door and sits back inside. As she settles in, I move. I'm still hidden from view but can see her through the driver's side window. She's staring down at the box and starts opening it. She lifts the top and sees a further note. I know what's on it. I printed it. I watch as she flicks on the phone's torch. I see her head move from side to side as she reads:

> Mike told me how you used to like a line yourself. Here's a present not to be shared with new friends. A gift Mike personally endorses. Hope to work together in the future. Enjoy the ride.

She stops reading, picks up the block, and begins to lightly caress the top. She's smiling as she holds the parcel closer to her. She turns and sees me.

'Sam,' she says, 'you shouldn't have.'

I get in the passenger seat and rack the seat back to allow for my leg length. We're alone. She carries on smoothing the block's wrapping, pleased with her acquisition.

'How are you keeping?' I say.

'Very well, as it goes. How did you know I was talking to the police?'

'Intuition and the fact that they have poor tradecraft,' I say.

She looks into my eyes. The grief I'd seen at the funeral has all disappeared. She reaches across and places both hands either side of my cheeks. She smells amazing.

She kisses me lightly on the lips, then sits back. I can taste strawberry lip balm and crave more. This was never the arrangement, though.

'I won't tell them about you. My lips are sealed,' she says.

I knew she'd be approached by our lot. After watching Mike's video, I knew she'd talk. She needs the money. She's used to a certain lifestyle and cocaine isn't easy to come by when your regular supplier becomes extinct. Why they'd go to her place of work is beyond me.

'What will you do now, Sam? Nick me with this parcel so you appear like you were innocent all along? Bent cop and cop's wife brought to justice by the mighty Sam

Batford? I wouldn't blame you if you did.' She gets out a cigarette and accepts my offer of a light.

The Sig Sauer pistol rests easy at the base of my back. The secluded environment a helpful location to ease my mind at what I must do.

'The note's an interesting touch, I must say. You might want to get rid of that.' She sits back and blows smoke out of the open window. A light breeze catches the strands of her hair. As she shifts them from her face, I can see her hand shaking.

'You know what happens to those that grass, don't you, Yvonne? Or whatever name you've been given to use now.'

Tears form in her eyes as she carries on smoking.

'Mike told me what would happen if I ever turned against him, so yeah, I do know. But what am I supposed to do? They know that I have information that would be useful. I felt I couldn't say no. I figured I could spin them along with some local dealers and hope they get bored.' She looks away. 'So, what's with the parcel of cocaine? One last line before I die? Is that it, Sam? Is that the extent of your good nature? I'm not going to argue. I know there's little point. You may as well get it over with. Do what you must, but let me at least finish the smoke before you do, hey?' She looks back at me. Her eyes are red in the dim light of the Fiat's interior. The glow from the full moon illuminates our surroundings.

'Why'd you kiss me?' I say.

'Because I can, now Mike has gone. I know he had other women, but I never cheated on him. Never. Call it a quick goodbye if you like.' She gets out another cigarette.

The time has come to do what I must do. I check around the outside of the car park. It's still deserted. She's put the parcel of cocaine on the central armrest.

'You work for me now,' I start. 'You don't work for Winter or the two source handlers she's referred you to. You will tell them what I want you to tell them and when I tell you to. In return, I will keep you in the lifestyle you want. That's it.'

She looks at me intently as she takes a long draw of smoke. The windows are up, and we enjoy the moment. A smile breaks across her face.

'That's it? I stay in touch with them, tell you what they're asking, and you keep me comfortable? I thought you were here to kill me. What if I say no?' she says, blowing a plume of smoke in my direction.

I retrieve the pistol from behind me.

'If you don't do what I ask, or double cross me, then you're not the person I thought you were, Yvonne.'

Her eyes don't leave the pistol. I lean towards her. She blinks.

'We both deserve a fresh start, don't we? It'd be a shame to waste what Mike built,' I say.

I put my hand on her neck and run it down her back. She doesn't resist. My hand drops, slowly, exploring her back, and each side of her body down to her waist. She's clean, no wires. Her body's taut from time in the gym. She reaches down to her handbag and brings out her phone to show me it's switched off. She opens her bag for good measure, showing me it's her only one.

'What happened to you, Sam?'

'Life is what happened.'

She puts the parcel of cocaine in her bag and turns towards me.

I put the gun in my waistband.

'What now?' she says.

I open the door and start getting out. 'I'll be in touch. Stay in contact and enjoy the package.'

She's smiling. All the tension gone. I feel I can trust her. Her need for ready access to cocaine is greater than Winter's need to see me imprisoned. I'm no good to her inside. Yvonne has clients who will expect continued supply and she'll value that more than anything Winter or the Professional Standards unit could promise her.

'One last thing,' I say, ducking down before I shut the door.

She leans across the passenger seat so she can hear me.

'I've taken care of Mike's ashes. He's in a place he valued and somewhere you both enjoyed visiting. Thought you should know.'

She asks nothing more as I shut the door and walk back towards the Tesla.

I get back in the Tesla, remove my gloves and, with one final check, leave.

Where's Mike? Yvonne will be closer to him with every line she snorts.

If you enjoyed this book, please let others know by leaving a quick review on Amazon. Also, if you spot anything untoward in the paperback, get in touch. We strive for the best quality and appreciate reader feedback.

editor@thebookfolks.com

www.thebookfolks.com

Also in this series

CRIMINAL JUSTICE (Book 1)

Batford walks a thin line when he infiltrates a criminal
gang. He sees an opportunity to make some money and
take down a pretty nasty felon, but his own boss
DCI Klara Winter is on to him. Can he get out of a very
sticky situation before his identity and intentions are
revealed?

STATUS DRIFT (Book 2)

DCI Klara Winter is out to get undercover officer Sam
Batford, convinced that he is corrupt and thwarted a
previous investigation for his own gain. During a new
operation in which Batford infiltrates a criminal network,
she lays a trap for him. But with a gangland boss after him,
that's the least of the rogue detective's worries.

All FREE with Kindle Unlimited and available in paperback!

More fiction by the author

LONDON CRIMES, the gripping police procedural series about detectives Pippa Nash and Nick Moretti.

LATENT DAMAGE (Book 1)

When a respected member of the community is murdered, it is not the kind of knife crime London detectives DI Nash and DS Moretti are used to dealing with. Someone has an agenda and it is rotten to the core. But catching this killer will take all of their police skills and more.

COVER BLOWN (Book 2)

A London advertising executive is found dead in her bath. Soon another woman is killed in similar circumstances. DI Nash and DS Moretti are hunting a killer, but finding a link between the victims is the only lead. What is it about their social media accounts that makes them a target?

SHOTS FIRED (Book 3)

After going cold, a London murder case suddenly reignites when the weapon used is connected to murders in Glasgow and Belfast. DI Nash and DS Moretti investigate but come under criticism. Nash will have to go out on a limb but will Moretti defend her?

EVIDENCE POOL (Book 4)

When a powerful Russian oligarch finds his assistant's lifeless body in his London mansion's pool, he is quick to claim diplomatic immunity and scurry into the panic room. Detectives Nash and Moretti are convinced the killer is still in the luxury residence, so they place the building on lockdown. But it seems that all of the members of the household, family and staff alike, have something to hide.

All FREE with Kindle Unlimited and available in paperback!

Other titles of interest

THE OTHER DETECTIVE
by James Davidson

Days before World War Two, Polish detective Johann Tal is called out to investigate a brutal murder. A couple have been discovered dead in Danzig's dockyards, and a policeman's bloodied uniform found next to them. Many years later, another detective is called out to a different murder. If the two cases are linked, it spells serious danger.

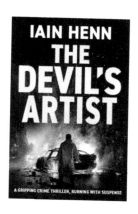

THE DEVIL'S ARTIST
by Iain Henn

When a massive wreck on the interstate kills several people, a mural in Seattle that seems to glorify the disaster creates outcry. However, upon discovering that the painting was created days before the event, criminal investigators are baffled. Are they dealing with a psychic artist, or someone who played a role in the incident? Soon other murals appear, and the race is on to stop further tragedy.

FREE with Kindle Unlimited and available in paperback!

Sign up to our mailing list to find out about new releases and special offers!

www.thebookfolks.com

Printed in Great Britain
by Amazon